AN INTRUDER IN THE NIGHT

The window flap seemed to explode inward. One instant it was intact, the next the grizzly's head was thrust inside the cabin, its rending teeth reducing the rawhide flap to strips and bits.

Nate's blood froze in his veins. He heard Evelyn scream as she flung herself away from the beast's wide maw, which was about to enfold her.

Then Winona was there. Seizing Evelyn by the shoulders, Winona pulled her beyond reach of the grizzly's gnashing teeth. They fell to the floor, Winona clasping Evelyn to her, as the bear roared in foiled frustration.

Nate drew his other pistol. The bear was clawing at the window in a frenzied attempt to force its way inside. He aimed squarely at the great head, and fired. At that range he could not miss. The ball struck the grizzly squarely between the eyes and dug a furrow in its fur but glanced off its thick skull and imbedded itself in the jamb.

All that achieved was to make the grizzly madder.

The *Wilderness* series:

#48
WILDERNESS
LORD GRIZZLY

David Thompson

LEISURE BOOKS NEW YORK CITY

Dedicated to Judy, Joshua and Shane.

A LEISURE BOOK®

April 2006

Published by

Dorchester Publishing Co., Inc.
200 Madison Avenue
New York, NY 10016

ISBN 0-8439-5461-2

Printed in the United States of America.

Visit us on the web at www.dorchesterpub.com.

LORD GRIZZLY

Prologue

The bear sniffed the air and growled at the scent carried to its sensitive nose by the warm summer breeze. It did not like the smell. It was the odor of the strange two-legged creatures who covered themselves with deer hides and were always doing things the bear could not fathom. Usually, the bear avoided the two-legs. At other times, it showed its displeasure by driving them off.

Once, when some two-legs spooked a doe and fawn the bear had stalked, it charged, roaring. The two-legs had fled astride the four-legged creatures they often rode. But not before one of the creatures held a thin stick to a larger curved stick, and the thin stick flew like a bird and glanced off the bear's shoulder. There was fleeting pain and some blood, but the wound was not serious. It taught the bear an important lesson, though.

The two-legs were puny, but they were dangerous.

After that, the bear wanted nothing to do with them,

and whenever it came across fresh two-leg sign, it went the other way.

But now that was not possible.

The two-legs had come to the bear's valley.

From a ridge high on a thickly timbered slope, the bear sniffed and glared at tendrils of smoke rising toward the sky from below, and a growl rumbled from deep within its huge chest.

This valley was special. It was the bear's home. It was where its mother had once had her den, and where the bear now had its own. No matter how far the bear ranged in its wide travels, it always came back.

The bear vaguely remembered its mother. It remembered wonderful warmth and feeling safe and content.

Then came the first cold the bear ever felt, and white fluff that fell from the clouds and piled so high, it rose to its mother's head and shoulders. They slept much during the cold, the mother and the bear, and when at last the mother ventured from the den, finding things to eat proved harder than it had ever been.

Of all the memories the bear had, the memory seared most vividly into its brain was the morning its mother led it across a white slope toward a stand of thin trees bare of leaves. They were halfway across when there was a loud sound from above, a crackling and a hissing like the crawlers made, only this had been much louder, and when the bear looked up, a white wall was rushing toward them. A wall that grew in size and sound as it hurtled nearer.

The bear's mother had whirled and pushed with her great head, trying to goad her cub into going back the way they had come. The bear sensed her fear, and was afraid. Although it ran as fast as it could, it kept slipping and falling.

Then its mother uttered a cry unlike any the bear ever heard her make, and the next instant the white wall was upon them. The rest was confusion. The bear tumbled end over end. White stuff filled its nose and choked its mouth, and there was a time when all was dark.

Cold woke the bear. Cold so great, it shivered and gnashed its teeth. It was surrounded by white, and when it breathed, more white filled its nose and its mouth. In a panic, the bear lashed out with its claws. Sudden brightness made it blink and squint. Sweet air filled its lungs, and it scrambled out of a white mound to find itself at the bottom of the mountain.

There was no sign of its mother. The bear bawled and bawled but she did not come, and that scared it worse than anything because there had never been a time when its mother did not rush to its side when it called for her.

The bear gazed up the slope and beheld a wondrous thing. Where before the lower part had been covered with trees, now almost all the trees were gone, swept away as if by a giant paw. Where the trees had stood was a white hill where there had not been a hill earlier.

Since the bear had last seen its mother higher up, the bear started up the mountain. It had not gone far when it came on the jagged trunk of a tree that poked above the white. Here and there other broken trees jutted skyward, their branches and needles stripped by the force of the cataclysm.

The bear struggled on through the drifts. Soon it was tired and damp and longing more than ever for its mother.

A new scent brought the bear to a halt. This was a scent it had smelled many times when its mother made a kill; the scent of blood. There were few things the bear liked to do more than lap up fresh blood or bite into juicy flesh dripping with blood.

The smell brought the bear to a stop. Tilting its head, it sniffed to one side and then to the other, doing as its mother would do when she was trying to locate prey. The scent was stronger to the bear's right.

Its stomach grumbling with hunger, the bear sought the source. Ahead was a shattered pine. Beside it was a white hump. From under the hump a red stain slowly spread.

The bear stopped, overcome by a terror it could not explain. It edged warily forward until it saw a paw much larger than its own. Whining in alarm, the bear dashed to the hump and pawed at the white stuff.

That was the day the bear's life forever changed. The day when it stared in mute misery at the still figure of its mother. A jagged limb had impaled her, ripping through her throat and up into her head. One eye had popped from its socket and hung by a strand. Where the eye had been was the gore-coated end of the limb.

The small bear nuzzled her and nipped at her forepaw, but its mother had not stirred. Whimpering, it lay beside her and waited for her to get up and show him what to do. But the day dragged by and its mother did not move.

All through that night the bear had stayed with her. The cold worsened, as it always did when the sun went down, and the bear snuggled next to her for warmth. But she had no warmth to share. She was a block of ice.

By sunrise the bear was colder than it had ever been.

4

It nudged its mother with its nose but she did not respond. She did not press her body to his and lick him as she always did.

Gradually it dawned on the bear that its mother would never rise. That she was now the same as the fish and deer and small creatures she had so often slain to fill their bellies.

Its mother was gone.

That first winter without her had been awful. The bear almost didn't survive to see the spring. But gradually it grew until it was as huge as she had been. Ultimately, it surpassed her.

In the fullness of its prime and its power, the bear roamed the mountains where it willed, doing what it pleased, when it pleased. It traveled over a large area, as its kind were wont to do, but it always returned to the special valley. It always came back to where its memories of its mother were strongest.

And now that special place had been violated.

Two-legs had come before. They never stayed, though. The bear saw to that, just as it would see to it that the new two-legs left.

The acrid scent of the smoke added to the bear's anger. Opening its great maw, it was about to roar its challenge, but did not. The two-legs would hear, and it was best when stalking to not let prey know it was being stalked.

The bear padded lower. When it wanted to, it could move as silently as the whispering wind, and it wanted to now.

The two-legs who had invaded its home must be driven off or slain, but the bear was in no hurry.

It had all the time in the world.

5

Chapter One

Nate King was happy. Happier than he had been in a coon's age. It had been so long since he was truly and genuinely happy that he had nearly forgotten how wonderful it felt.

Nate had a lot to be happy about. He and his loved ones had arrived at the remote valley, deep in the Rocky Mountains, that was to be their new home. With him were his wife, Winona, a full-blooded Shoshone, and their daughter, Evelyn. Also along were Nate's son, Zach, and Zach's wife, Louisa. Nor was that all. Nate's best friend in all creation, famed frontiersman Shakespeare McNair, and Shakespeare's lovely Flathead wife, Blue Water Woman, completed their party.

In Nate's opinion the move to the new valley was long overdue. Their old cabin had been too close to the foothills. It had become a stopping-off point for every settler and adventurer on their way into the high country. To say nothing of less savory sorts, cutthroats of every stripe who had fled civilization a few steps ahead of a noose and came to the mountains to escape.

The Utes were also a factor. For years Nate had enjoyed an uneasy truce with the tribe. Many of the Utes, especially the younger ones, resented his presence in their territory. He was a white man, and the Utes had good reason to mistrust whites. Nate had also been adopted into the Shoshones, and the Utes and the Shoshones were not on friendly terms.

The Crows were not fond of Nate, either. Not long ago, his son had blown holes in a lot of Crow skulls to stop a war between the Crows and the Shoshones, and the Crows held Nate to blame as much as Zach.

Then there was the white woman who had abducted Nate's daughter and nearly sold her into a life of lechery.

Additional proof, as if any were needed, that it was high time Nate pulled up roots and relocated. He had been thinking about it for a long time. But he kept putting it off, kept telling himself he would do it next week, or the week after that. Months went by, and still he procrastinated. But no more. Evelyn's kidnaping had been like a bucket of ice-cold water thrown in his face.

Now Nate stood on the shore of a pristine lake in the center of the new valley and raised his hands to the surrounding peaks. "Take a look! It is beautiful here, don't you think?"

"I reckon it is, Horatio," Shakespeare McNair agreed. The white-haired gentleman had two quirks: one, he was passionately fond of the Bard, after whom he was nicknamed, and he could recite his namesake by the hours; and two, he liked to call Nate after characters in the Bard's masterful plays. "But it was right pretty where I lived before." Shakespeare sighed. "How I let you talk me into this, I will never savvy."

"Do not listen to him," Blue Water Woman said in English. "In his old age, he complains as much as a woman."

"Did my ears deceive me?" Shakespeare put a hand to his chest in a mock show of being grievously hurt. "If she lives till doomsday she will burn a week longer than the whole world," he quoted.

Evelyn laughed and said, "I like it when you talk funny, Uncle Shakespeare. I always have."

"Talk funny?" Shakespeare repeated, aghast. "Oh illiterate loiterer. How prove you that in the great heap of your knowledge?"

"I think you have just been insulted, Evelyn," Blue Water Woman said.

"And I wasn't when you called me an old woman?" Shakespeare joked. "From the extremist upward of thy head to the descent and dust below thy foot, a most toad-spotted traitor."

"My, aren't you in a mood," Blue Water Woman held her own. "Just like a woman."

Nate laughed at their antics and strolled from their campfire to the water's edge. The lake was a vivid blue-green, in part because one of the streams that fed it brought runoff from a glacier. The water was so clear that Nate could see pebbles on the bottom, and a school of small fish that flitted past like so many aqueous hummingbirds.

"Can I talk to you, Pa?"

Nate had not heard his son approach. "Are you glad we are finally here, Zach? I am."

"I am glad that you are glad," Zach answered. "I only hope Louisa grows to like this place as much as she did our last home."

Nate did not need to be reminded that the move had been his idea. Zach and Shakespeare had taken a lot of convincing. Neither had wanted to relocate. Their wives had been perfectly pleased where they were. Nate persuaded them by stressing it was best for their mutual protection, if no other reason. "What's on your mind?"

"We have been here two days and have not done anything except lie around," Zach complained. "We should pick our cabin sites and start chopping trees."

"We have been lying around, as you call it," Nate said, "because we needed the rest." It had taken them weeks to get there, over some of the most rugged terrain in the Rockies. "But if it will make you feel better, tomorrow we scout around for sites."

"I just don't like twiddling my thumbs."

Nate smiled. His son had always been a bundle of vinegar and vim. "If you need something to do, venison for supper would be nice. I don't know about you, but I'm mighty tired of rabbit and squirrel."

"The first deer I see," Zach said, and started to turn.

"Keep your eyes skinned for sign," Nate advised. "Indians, wolves, cougars, you name it."

"What about bear?" Zach grinned. "Have you come to your senses yet? Or do you still intend to end your days as bear droppings?"

Nate was used to his family teasing him over his latest brainstorm. "No, I haven't changed my mind. Just because no one has ever done it doesn't mean it can't be done."

"And just because we don't have wings doesn't mean we can't fly," Zach quipped. Chuckling merrily, he sauntered toward the horses.

"No one takes me seriously," Nate sighed, and then saw his wife standing a few yards away. She had overheard.

"I take you seriously, Husband. You always speak with a straight tongue. When you say you will do something, you do it. Which is why I am worried. I do not care to live the rest of my life a widow." Winona, like Blue Water Woman, was fluent in the white man's tongue. Extraordinarily so. She took great pride in being able to speak it as well as Nate.

"Thanks for the confidence," he said dryly.

"I have always had confidence in you. Even when you were young and did not have confidence in yourself." Winona came over and placed a hand on his shoulder. "You know that."

Nate looked at her. With her flowing raven hair, smooth complexion and beaded buckskin dress, she was a true beauty. He had loved her from the moment he set eyes on her, and his love had grown over the years to where he could not live without her. "Then have it now."

Winona touched his cheek. "I have confidence you can shoot the head off a rattlesnake at ten paces. I have confidence you can hold your own against the Blackfeet or the Piegans or any other hostile tribe. I have confidence you can hunt any animal and track better than most men, white or red. In all this I have

11

confidence." Winona paused. "But you are asking me now to believe you can do something that has never been done before. You are asking me to have confidence in something that can get not only you killed, but the rest of us, as well."

"I would never put any of you in danger," Nate said, annoyed she would suggest such a thing.

"But you are," Winona responded. "The longer that grizzly is alive, the greater the risk it will kill one of us."

"No one can predict what a bear will do," Nate said, his irritation climbing. "Why is everyone making such a fuss over this? I'm only trying to do the right thing."

"Are you?" Winona asked. "Or is it that your conscience is bothering you so much, you have thrown common sense to the wind, as whites would say?"

"I don't know what you are talking about."

Winona lowered her hand and gazed off across the lake. "I take back what I said about you always speaking with a straight tongue. Because you do know what I am talking about. You earned the name my people call you, Grizzly Killer, the hard way. You have killed many silver-tips, Husband. More than anyone, ever. And because you have killed so many, and you are sick of the killing, you want to make amends by sparing the grizzly that lives in this valley."

Nate opened his mouth to disagree and then closed it again. She was right, and he knew it. He had slain a heap of grizzlies. But back then grizzlies were everywhere. They roamed the plains in great numbers. In the mountains they were legion. A trapper could hardly turn around without bumping into one. An exaggeration, perhaps, but not much of one. Could he help it if it had been his misfortune to bump into a lot of them? Worse, most of those he bumped into did not run off, but came after him with slavering jaws and bestial bloodlust in their ursine eyes. It was him or them, and he did not want it to be him.

Since then, their numbers had been reduced. A man could ride for days without seeing one. Nate hadn't needed to kill a griz in a good long while, and he would like to avoid killing any in the future.

On his first visit to this new valley, Nate had come across grizzly sign. In the old days he wouldn't have hesitated to track the bear down and slay it so it wouldn't pose a threat to his family. But this time he wanted to do things differently. This time he wanted to leave the grizzly alone if the grizzly would leave him and his alone. But it begged the crucial question: How did one go about convincing a mammoth eating machine not to eat potential prey?

As if Winona were privy to his innermost thoughts, she asked, "Have you figured out how you will do it? Bears are not dogs. They cannot be trained as you trained the wolf Zach had when he was little."

"How do we know that?" Nate stubbornly argued. "Has anyone ever tried to train a grizzly before?"

"Not and lived to tell about it," Winona said. "Once there was a Shoshone named Swift Antelope. He found a black bear cub in a hole in an old tree and brought it to the village. The elders were not pleased, but it was agreed he could keep the bear so long as the bear did not cause trouble."

Nate listened attentively. She always had a point to her stories, and he was fairly sure where this one would lead.

"The cub was friendly and adorable. Everyone

wanted to hold it and pet it. Swift Antelope kept it on a rope outside his lodge, and was kept busy finding enough for it to eat." Winona folded her arms across her bosom. "The cub grew fast. In a few winters it was many times the size it had been when Swift Antelope found it. It did not like being a pet anymore, and nipped at a few people who came too close."

"Let me guess," Nate said.

"Swift Antelope's friends advised him to take the black bear off into the woods but he refused to listen. He was too fond of it. He said he could teach it not to bite."

Nate interrupted with, "Teach it how?"

"Whenever the bear did something it should not do, Swift Antelope would raise his voice to it and with-hold its food."

"He never hit it?" Nate wasn't surprised. The Shoshones did not believe in physically punishing children, or animals. It had been hard for him to accept when Zach and Evelyn were young. His father had taken him to the woodshed many a time, and he had turned out just fine.

"He never hit it," Winona confirmed. "The bear behaved, for a while. It did not bite or growl. Then one day Swift Antelope brought it a bowl of berries, and as he set the bowl down, the black bear clawed him across the arm."

"You saw it?"

"I was not there, but my cousin saw the whole thing from her lodge. She said Swift Antelope spoke sternly to the bear, and bent down to pick up the bowl. The bear tried to claw him again but Swift Antelope backed away. He told the bear that it could have the berries if it wanted. But the bear, being a bear, did not understand. And being a bear, it did the last thing Swift Antelope expected. It bit through the rope and attacked him."

"Right there in the village?"

Winona nodded. "Swift Antelope tried to fight it off without hurting it or letting it hurt him, but the bear was too big, and it slashed his chest and his legs. He was bleeding badly and drew his knife to defend himself. The bear bit him in the leg, so he stabbed it. By then others were running to help but before they could reach him, the black bear knocked him down and sank its teeth in his throat. He died horribly. And the bear, the cute little bear he had raised from a cub, started to eat him. Touch the Clouds killed it with three arrows."

"I am not Swift Antelope," Nate said.

"No, you are not," Winona replied. "But when you talk of training a grizzly, I think of him, and I am very afraid. You can not train that which cannot be trained. And I do not care to be a widow."

Zach King rode west out of camp. He was glad to be on his own for a while. As much as he loved Louisa, and he truly did, and as fond as he was of his family, even his sister, he enjoyed getting away to hunt.

Since this was his first visit to the valley, Zach studied it intently. The lake was like a giant blue pupil at the center of a giant green eye. The valley floor was lush with grass. Wildflowers in the form of meadow daises and columbines were abundant. Every adjoining slope was densely timbered with spruce, fir and pine. Willows grew along one of the streams. Higher up were stands of aspens.

Several of the encircling peaks wore caps of white snow. To the northwest, near the crown of the highest mountain, was the glacier. Zach made a promise to himself that one day he would ride up there and touch it.

In such a verdant valley, it was only natural that there would be plenty of animal sign, but Zach was still surprised at how much he discovered. Deer appeared to be as numerous as blades of grass. He saw the larger hoofprints of elk and even a few prints made by mountain buffalo. Along a game trail he found tracks of coyotes, porcupines and skunks.

Zach was delighted to spy an otter slide on the bank of the stream. As a boy he had often watched otters at play, wishing he could be as carefree as they were. Farther along he came on a sight he had not beheld in many months: a beaver dam. Thanks to the demand for plews during the beaver craze of a decade ago, the beaver population was lower than it had ever been, and their dams few and extremely far between. He could not wait to tell his father.

Past the dam was the pond, and beyond that a hummock sprinkled with cinquefoils. Zach climbed to a slope heavy with blue spruce and threaded among stately trees. He saw calypso, surprising at that altitude although not unheard of, and some heartleaf.

A log barred his way and Zach reined the zebra dun around it. On top of the log was raccoon scat, some recent, some old. Raccoons tended to follow the same path night after night, and was the only animal Zach knew of that did its business on fallen trees.

At that time of the day, the deer were holed up deep

in the brush. They would rest until twilight, then come out to graze.

Zach roved in a wide loop, seeking fresh sign. He found it on a grassy spine below a ridge. Several deer had grazed there that morning and then gone off into the undergrowth. He fingered the Hawken rifle cradled in the crook of his left elbow. Like his father and McNair, he was a virtual armory. In addition to the rifle, he had twin flintlocks wedged under his leather belt on either side of the brass buckle. On his right hip hung a hunting knife, on his left a tomahawk. Slanted across his chest were his ammo pouch, powder horn and possibles bag. Buckskins and moccasins completed the portrait.

The deer tracks were easy to follow. Zach had learned from masters. His father and Shakespeare were superbly skilled. McNair alone had lived in the mountains for more than fifty years, and his store of woodlore was second to none.

Zach had gone a short distance when the spacing of the tracks changed. Where before they were about two feet apart, the typical walking gait for deer, now the prints were six and seven feet apart, or more. Which told Zach the deer had bolted and bounded up the slope as if in fear for their lives.

An explanation was soon forthcoming.

Zach came to a small tract of bare soil, and there, clearly imprinted, was the mark of a mountain lion's front paw. He estimated the width at close to four inches. As was typical with cat tracks, the claws did not show. He made a mental note to tell his father when he returned.

In the old valley, Nate had killed every predator that posed a threat to their family or their livestock: every bear, every wolf, every mountain lion. What his father would do about this new cat, Zach could not guess.

His father had changed. Zach could not say exactly when the change took place, but his father had a different view of things. Foremost was the notion that grizzlies and men could live in peace.

To Zach it was absurd. Grizzlies were meat eaters, and they did not care where the meat came from. Grizzlies killed whatever they could catch. Nothing was safe, not elk, not black bear, not even buffalo. Zach once witnessed a tremendous battle between a bull buffalo and a griz that ended with the griz feasting on the buff's remains.

To tell the truth, Zach was worried about his father. A man must never let down his guard in the wilderness, never give other men or beasts the benefit of the doubt. It was kill or be killed, the law of fang and claw. Men survived by the grace of cold steel and lead, a truth Zach had learned at an early age. His father once lived by that truth. Now Nate wanted to live in peace with all things, as peculiar a notion as anyone ever had.

Zach shook himself. Here he was, with a mountain lion in the vicinity, and he was thinking about his father when he should be as alert as a honed razor. Hefting his Hawken, he rode higher.

The tracks told the rest of the story.

The frightened deer had scattered, seeking to lose their feline pursuer. But the mountain lion had already selected its victim and veered after one deer in particular. By the tracks it was smallest, which meant it was the youngest, and the youngest were invariably the slowest.

The end came swiftly. Within twenty yards the big cat had overtaken its quarry, and sprang. In his mind's eye Zach envisioned what happened next; the lion landed on the deer's back, its weight crashing the doe to earth as its fangs sheared into her head, crushing her skull as a vise might crush an eggshell. The doe had been dead when she struck the ground, or close to it. A few feeble twitches, and it was all over.

Suddenly the zebra dun nickered. Zach drew rein. A dozen yards away was a pile of needles. From under it poked two slender legs. Around it was a pool of dried blood. The cat had cached its kill and gone off to sleep.

Or had it? Zach wondered. Sometimes mountain lions stayed close to their kills, and would attack anything, or anyone, that came near it. He gigged the zebra dun to go around the pile.

A hint of movement off among the spruce caused Zach to rein up. Tucking the Hawken's stock to his shoulder, he probed the shadows. If the cat attacked, he might get off a shot before it reached him. He must not miss.

Tense moments ensued as Zach waited for the mountain lion to show itself. But nothing happened. He was about convinced it was safe to ride on when out of the corner of his eye he registered movement. Shifting in the saddle, he fixed a hasty bead on a quicksilver form and thumbed back the hammer. He didn't shoot, though.

The cougar was racing eastward, a tawny streak against the backdrop of green and brown, taking long leaps that put those of any other creature to shame. In seconds it had covered fifty yards, and stopped and looked back. Flattening its ears, its sinewy tail twitching, the mountain lion snarled and bared its fangs.

Zach had the cat squarely in his sights. He told himself he should shoot, that the lion might one day decide horseflesh was tastier than deer flesh or human flesh was tastier than both. But he thought of his father, and relaxed his trigger finger.

With another snarl, the cougar bounded into the vegetation.

"That was stupid," Zach chided himself.

Suddenly the zebra dun reared and whinnied. Zach clamped his legs against the saddle and held on to keep from falling. He could not understand why the horse was acting so frightened when the mountain lion was gone. Then he heard a rumbling growl, and had his answer.

The cougar had not been fleeing from him. It had been running from something else. Something far more formidable.

Out of the undergrowth reared the grizzly.

Chapter Two

The *thunk* of axes biting into wood thudded in a steady cadence. Winona tilted her head to listen, and smiled at the thought that in another month she would have a roof over her head again. A solid log roof, supported by log walls, protection against the elements and beasts alike.

Winona would never admit it to her Shoshone relatives and friends, but she liked living in a cabin more than she did a traditional Shoshone lodge. It had not always been the case.

When Nate took her as his mate, living in his uncle's cabin had taken a lot of getting used to. The cabin had been as gloomy as a cave, the walls so thick that being inside was like being entombed in solid rock. In a cabin, unlike a lodge, she could not hear what was going on outside. She could not hear the wind unless it

David Thompson

was especially strong. Whenever it rained, she missed the familiar patter of drops.

Gradually her outlook changed. Winona came to appreciate the security the thick log walls offered. She equally liked the extra protection the roof afforded from downpours and snowstorms.

Most of all, Winona had relished the cozy feeling she got when she sat in her rocking chair in front of the stone fireplace, either warmed by crackling flames in the winter or cooled by the gentle breeze that always wafted in the open window on a summer's eve.

The extra space in the cabin was another plus, as was the privacy of having their own bedroom.

Small wonder, then, that Winona could not wait for their new cabin to be built so they could settle in and resume the everyday rhythm of their lives.

Hunkered by a travois, Winona was searching for a hairbrush Nate had bought for her at Bent's Fort when a shadow fell across her.

"My silly excuse for a husband says I can pick our cabin site," Blue Water Woman announced. "Care to go along?"

Winona hesitated. She had a lot of work to do but the invitation was tempting.

"Come on," Blue Water Woman urged. "We can use some time to ourselves. The girls said they would go if you did."

That news decided things for Winona. Over the past few months she could count on two hands the number of minutes she spent alone with her daughter or her daughter-in-law. "Count me in."

Evelyn and Louisa were saddling the horses. Winona

noticed that her mare was already ready to go. "How did you know I would agree?"

"I'm not your offspring for nothing, Ma," Evelyn joked. "Besides, Pa said if you didn't agree, I was to drag you along."

"He did, did he?" Winona glanced toward the forest but could not see the love of her life because of the intervening trees.

"Pa said it would do us biddy hens good to gab awhile," Evelyn said. "His exact words."

"Remind me to talk to him about that," Winona grinned. "Right after I beat him with a frying pan."

"Men!" Blue Water Women said. "We can't live without them, and we can't throw them off cliffs."

Louisa was cinching her mount. "There are days when I would like to heave Zach off a cliff, let me tell you. He can be the most pigheaded man alive."

"The second most pigheaded," Blue Water Woman said. "Shakespeare is solid pig between his ears."

They all laughed, then climbed on their horses and rode south around the lake at a leisurely pace. The sun was warm on their faces, the wind caressed their hair. Out in the water a large fish arced into the air and slapped down with a loud splash. Far across the lake several doe ventured out of the woods to slake their thirst.

"I sure do like it here, Ma," Evelyn said. On the cusp of womanhood, she sat her saddle tall and straight, her young eyes aglow with the vitality of life. "Pa had the right idea, didn't he?"

"Time will tell," Winona said.

"It's a mite scary for me," Louisa admitted. Unlike

them, she cropped her hair short, and looked almost boyish in her buckskins. "We're a lot deeper in the mountains than we were."

And a lot farther from Shoshone country, Winona thought to herself. A lot farther from the only tribe they could count on if they needed help.

"I do not care where I live so long as I am with Shakespeare," Blue Water Woman said. "We were joined late in life and have a lot of catching up to do."

Winona knew the details. How they had met when they were young and been very much in love, but circumstances conspired to separate them until many years later. How sad, she reflected, that some people could go nearly their entire lives without their one and only. She could not bear to think of life without Nate. He was everything to her. Their hearts were as one, and would forever be entwined.

"I am in no hurry to get married, I can tell you that," Evelyn was saying.

"Oh?" Louisa winked at Winona. "With all the suitors you have?"

Evelyn blushed a bright crimson. "Don't remind me. I've done everything but beat them off with a stick. They can't seem to take a hint."

The "them" she referred to were a young Crow, Chases Rabbits, and a young Ute, Niwot, who had come courting, much to Evelyn's astonishment, and Winona's displeasure. Even though it was customary for Indian girls to take husbands at an earlier age than most white girls, Winona was in no rush to see her daughter married off.

"Men never take hints," Blue Water Woman declared. "You must beat them with a rock, not a stick, or they will not notice."

"Zach is the same way," Louisa lamented. "Sometimes talking to him is like talking to a tree. It goes in one ear and bounces back out."

Winona had to chortle. "We all agree, then. Men are a trick Coyote has played on us."

"Or a torment," Blue Water Woman said.

"But their strong backs sure come in handy," Louisa said, "among other things."

They all laughed except Evelyn. Winona drew rein to admire the lake and the others followed her example. "I have been thinking about where to build my cabin, and I would like it near the shore, there." She pointed at the west end of the lake.

"Pa will never go for that," Evelyn said. "It's in the open. Anyone who happens by would see it."

Louisa encompassed the broad expanse of the valley with a gesture. "Who would happen by way out here in the middle of nowhere? I doubt there's another white person on earth who knows this valley exists."

"The Utes know about it, and not all the Utes are friendly," Evelyn said.

"But this is not Ute territory, like our last home," Winona interjected. "They have no reason to bother us here." The Utes lived to the southeast. To the northeast were Winona's own people, the Shoshones. To the north dwelled the Bannocks, haters of all things white. To the west and the southwest lay unknown territory. Winona had heard that a tribe called the Paiutes lived in the direction of the setting sun, but she knew little about them.

"Neither does the Blackfoot Confederacy," Blue Water Woman brought up. Consisting of the Blackfeet, the Piegans and the Bloods, the Confederacy held violent sway over the northern Rockies and plains. Occasionally, war parties penetrated south into Shoshone and Ute territory. But never this far.

Evelyn suddenly pointed at the lake. "What in blazes is that?"

Out in the middle a commotion was taking place. Long, rippling waves had appeared, growing longer by the instant as something cleaved the surface like the prow of a canoe. They glimpsed a dark object that resembled nothing so much as a submerged log. But a log that was alive, and moving faster than any fish.

"Lord Almighty!" Louisa blurted.

"It's huge," Evelyn declared.

The thing's wake widened, creating more waves. Winona wished she could see more of the creature making it. She judged it to be as long as two buffalo standing nose to tail but it might be bigger.

Suddenly, as abruptly as it had appeared, the dark shape disappeared. It simply sank out of sight. The waves continued to ripple, growing smaller with distance, until they swished ashore within a few yards of where the three women and the girl sat their mounts.

"That was the oddest critter I ever saw," Louisa commented.

"What do you think it was?" Evelyn asked. She was looking at Winona but it was Blue Water Woman who responded.

"Can it be? There are stories the old ones of my tribe tell. But I never imagined I would see proof."

"What stories?" Louisa prompted.

"Tell us about them," Evelyn requested.

Blue Water Woman was quiet a bit. Then she slowly began, "My people have tales of the early times. Of the world as it was when the first people appeared, and the creatures that lived in the world then."

"The Shoshones have stories like that too," Evelyn said.

"All tribes do," Blue Water Woman responded. "My people once believed that the world is an island, with water all around, in a giant hollow mountain."

"Really?" Evelyn giggled. "That's plain silly."

"Whites once believed the world was flat," Louisa said, "and that if a ship sailed to the end of the sea, it would fall off."

"That's even sillier," Evelyn observed. To Blue Water Woman she said, "Go on. Please."

"My tribe calls the creator of all things Amotken. He made the world and the first people. But they were bad in their hearts, so Amotken caused a great flood to wipe them out. He created a second race, larger and stronger than the first one, but they, too, were evil, so Amotken brought fire down on their heads, destroying them."

Winona spoke up. "The Shoshones say there was a great fire at the beginning of things. The Father of all and his wife and son walked through the flames. He told them not to look back at the fire but his wife did not listen and looked, and was turned to stone."

Louisa gave a start. "That's mighty peculiar. There's a story in the Bible where Lot's wife looked back when the Lord destroyed Sodom and Gomorrah with fire, and she was turned to stone. Just like in your story."

"Land sakes," Evelyn said.

Blue Water Woman went on. "Amotken did not give up. He created a third race of people, bigger than the first two. They were giants. But they—"

"Giants?" Louisa interrupted. "There is a mention of giants in the Bible! But I don't recollect the particulars."

"They were as wicked as all the rest," Blue Water Woman related, "so Amotken destroyed them, too."

"How?" Evelyn asked. "Did he drown them or burn them up?"

"Neither. He destroyed them with a disease," Blue Water Woman related. "Even though three races had been wicked, Amotken did not give up. He made a fourth race. But he was not happy with them and would have destroyed them, as well. His mother talked him out of it. She said he should give the new race a chance."

"Finally," Louisa said. "Say, what does Amotken mean, anyway?"

"The Great Spirit Above, or the Great Mystery," Blue Water Woman translated. "There is a story that once, so long ago it is lost in the mists of age, Amotken appeared on earth as a white man to teach us how to do things. How to make bows and hunt and live off the land."

"Wait a second," Louisa broke in. "Did you say a white man?"

"Yes. It is why, when the first white men came to our land, my people thought they were from Amotken, and could not be killed. They were greatly shocked when one was slain by the Blackfeet."

"This fourth race of people you mentioned," Evelyn said, "were they us?"

"No. They were the animal people. Animals who

28

could walk and talk and think like we do," Blue Water Woman said. "One of them was Coyote. My people have more stories about him than anyone else."

"The Shoshones, too, have many stories about Coyote," Winona mentioned.

"But what does all this have to do with the thing we just saw in the lake?" Louisa asked.

Blue Water Woman solemnly regarded the now placid surface. "The Flatheads believe that in the early times there were many monsters in the world. Monsters of the land and of the water. They were very bad medicine."

Evelyn giggled. "No one believes in monsters these days."

"Maybe they should," Blue Water Woman said in all seriousness. "There is always some truth to the old stories. When the elders say there were monsters in the early times, believe them. And when the elders say some of those monsters are still alive, we should believe that, too. For we have witnessed the evidence with our own eyes."

"You're saying that thing we saw was a monster?" Louisa said. "That can't be."

Blue Water Woman shrugged. "Who of us can say what is and what is not? The early times were not like our times. The animal people were not like us. The other creatures were not like the creatures that live now." She gazed at the azure sky and a white cloud drifting overheard. "There is more to the world than what we see with our eyes and hear with our ears."

"Tell us more about the monsters," Evelyn coaxed.

"There were different kinds. There were snakes that could fly, and giant fish, and monsters with the head of a horse and the body of a snake that could crush a man in their coils." Blue Water Woman gestured. "The horse-head monsters lived in lakes like this one."

A silence fell, a silence so heavy that the sigh of the wind and the lap of a few tiny ripples seemed unnaturally loud.

"The Shoshones have tales of monsters, too," Winona said. "In Bull Lake there once lived water buffalo. They would come out on land to lie in the sun and play. One day two hunters saw them, and killed one. They skinned the water buffalo, and butchered it, and roasted it for their supper. But as they were eating, a strange thing happened. Their bodies did not feel right. They looked down at themselves and saw their feet change into hoofs. Horns sprouted on their heads. They jumped up, afraid, but it was too late for them. They turned into water buffalo."

Louisa laughed. "That's ridiculous. But no more so than some of the fairy tales whites like to share."

"The monsters of the old times are not fairy tales," Blue Water Woman said. "They killed many people, and were hard to kill, in turn. One of the worst was the giant snake monster that lived in what the whites call the Columbia River. As savage as could be, and always hungry, it ate everything that came near it until one day Coyote slew it."

"So how many of these monsters would you say are still around?" Evelyn nervously asked.

"No one can say. Many were killed. They drowned in the flood that covered the world."

"Your people have stories of a flood too?" Louisa marveled. "In the Bible there is a story about a man named Noah and a great flood. How can it be that both our peoples have the same story?"

"It makes one wonder," Blue Water Woman said.

Evelyn cleared her throat. "Surely you don't believe that the thing we saw was a water monster?"

"Who can say?"

Evelyn turned to Winona. "You don't believe it's a monster, do you, Ma?"

"It could be a big fish," Winona hedged. "I remember once when several warriors killed a fish nearly as big as their canoe."

"But what if it *is* a monster?" Louisa excitedly asked. "We should tell our menfolk. We can't settle here if we're going to have a monster for a neighbor."

"They would laugh at the notion, and at us," Winona predicted.

"What interests me is that your Great Spirit appeared to your people as a white man," Louisa said to Blue Water Woman, "long before Lewis and Clark came along."

"I have never known what to make of that," Blue Water Woman confessed. "Nor of the story about the Mystery People."

"The who?"

"That is the name the elders call them. This was very long ago, but after the time of the ice, when the Salish came down from the north—"

"The who?" From Louisa.

"My tribe," Blue Water Woman explained. "We call ourselves the Salish. Flathead is the white word."

"Please go on. What was that about ice?"

"Once most of the world was covered with ice.

31

There were many giant animals in those days. Hairy animals with long tusks and long teeth. The Salish did not like the cold, so they came south and settled near the big lake now known as Flathead Lake. The Salish were happy in their new home. Many winters passed, and then one day strangers came up the river in big canoes unlike any ever seen." Blue Water Woman paused. "The men in the canoes were not Indians and they were not whites. They were a new race. Smaller than the Salish, but very wise. The women in the canoes were all from coast tribes. The strange men had taken them for wives."

Winona was fascinated by the account. "Where did the strange men come from?"

"From far across the Great Salt Sea," Blue Water Woman revealed. "In a big canoe with sails. A storm had caught them and pushed them east until they did not know where they were. Then they came in sight of land, and it was the coast to the land the whites call Oregon Country. Their big canoe wrecked, and they could not go back. They became friends with the coast tribes, and married their women. Then they built new canoes and came in the direction of the rising sun up the great river until they came to Flathead Lake."

Louisa was scratching her head. "They must have come clear across the Pacific Ocean. Maybe they were Chinese or Japanese. Or from an island in the Pacific Ocean."

"Whoever they were, they were very friendly," Blue Water Woman said. "They built new homes on islands in the lake, and taught the Salish many things."

"Such as?" Louisa wanted to know.

"How to strike rocks together to make fire. How to

cure diseases with medicines made from leaves and roots. How to treat wounds," Blue Water Woman recited. "The Mystery People also taught the Salish that it was good to take baths, and that they must never throw old meat or anything bad near the water they drank as it could make them sick."

"All that?" Evelyn said.

"And more. The Salish thought them wonderful things. But there was one thing the Mystery Men did that the Salish could not understand. They flattened their heads, and those of their wives and their children."

Louisa arched an eyebrow. "They did what?"

"It was the custom among the Mystery People to press boards on the heads of infants and tie the boards fast so that their heads became flat at the top. Later, when the white man came to our territory, the whites saw a few of the last of the Mystery People, and their flat heads, and gave the Salish that name. But it was the Mystery People who had flat heads, not us."

"What happened to them?" Winona inquired.

"The first of the Mystery People grew old and died. Their children married Salish, and after many winters there were few Mystery People left. Now there are none," Blue Water Woman concluded.

Louisa was staring across the lake. "I still don't know what to make of that business about lake monsters. I only hope it was a giant fish we saw, and not one of those other critters."

"I just hope it doesn't slither out of the lake in the middle of the night and gobble us up," Evelyn said. She was joking but there was a hint of apprehension in her tone.

"I would worry more about the grizzly, were I you, daughter," Winona said. The thought of what the bear might do to her husband if he went through with his plan to try and tame it had given her sleepless nights.

"You know, I just realized something," Louisa said, twisting in her saddle to scan the valley rim. "I don't recall coming across any bear tracks on our way in. Did any of you?"

Winona had to think. The valley was a gigantic bowl ringed by mountainous ramparts. The only way in was through a canyon to the east, and not once on the ride up it had she seen so much as a single grizzly print. "No, I did not. Nor many elk or deer tracks, either."

"Then there must be another way in and out," Louisa deduced. "A pass, maybe, high up on one of the peaks."

"A secret way we do not know about yet?" Winona hoped her daughter-in-law was wrong. For if there was a secret pass, and hostile tribes knew of it, they could all be in great danger.

"As soon as our cabins are built, Zach and I will go have a look-see," Louisa proposed. "There is nothing he likes more than exploring new country."

"Nothing?" Blue Water Woman said, and she and Louisa laughed.

"He likes chocolate a lot," Evelyn commented. "When we were little he had a sweet tooth the size of Long's Peak. He was always licking his finger and dipping it in the sugar bowl."

Louisa and Blue Water Woman laughed harder.

"What did I say?" Evelyn quizzically asked Winona. "He did so have a sweet tooth. You remember, don't you?"

At that juncture, from far off and high up, there came the distant crack of a gunshot. Winona cocked her head, sure it had been a rifle. "That must be Zach. We will have roast venison tonight."

Hardly half a minute went by when there was another shot, slightly fainter than the first.

"That was a pistol," Louisa said. "He must have had to finish the deer off." She added with pride, "Usually it only takes him one."

No sooner were the words out of her mouth than there was a third crack, much like the second.

"His rifle and both pistols on one deer?" Louisa said skeptically. "That's not like Zach. That's not like him at all."

Winona reined her horse around. "We must go back."

"What is it, Ma?" Evelyn asked.

"Probably nothing," Winona said. But deep in her being she was convinced otherwise. Deep in her being she believed that something was very, very wrong.

Chapter Three

Zach King had seen plenty of grizzly bears. Male grizzlies, female grizzlies, old grizzlies, young grizzlies, big grizzlies, small grizzlies. But it was safe to say he had never seen one as immense as the grizzly that reared before him. It seemed to be as tall as the trees, an illusion fostered by the sun at its back, and the fact the bear was twenty feet higher on the slope.

Zach fought an impulse to bolt. Over short distances a grizzly could outrun a horse. The wise move was to sit quietly and hope the bear lost interest and wandered elsewhere. The zebra dun stamped a front hoof and bobbed its head but did not flee, much to Zach's surprise.

The great bear regarded them both with inscrutable intent. By Zach's best reckoning it had to weigh well over a thousand pounds. Probably close to twelve hundred. More than half a ton of iron muscle and steely bone. Half a tone of the most formidable carnivore on the continent, armed with four-inch claws and teeth nearly as long, a living, breathing, behemoth, the master of its domain. Lord grizzly, the true king of beasts, against whom no creature could stand.

Zach never ceased to marvel that his father had killed so many of the giant bears. Many a time he had asked Nate how it happened, and each time his father gave him the same answer: dumb luck.

Now, staring up into the dark pools of latent ferocity that were the grizzly's eyes, Zach recalled the stories he had heard about their remarkable endurance and prowess. How the Lewis and Clark expedition shot one fourteen times, and the grizzly would still not go down. How an entire Ute village was held captive to fear for months because of a grizzly's raids. How a Shoshone warrior named Drags The Rope once saw a grizzly fight three large black bears at the same time, and the black bears lost.

Zach also remembered a tale told by the Shoshone elders. How at one time there had been other bears that roamed the mountains. Bears even larger than grizzlies. Bears that shook the ground when they walked.

Then there was the Father Of All Bears, the greatest bruin of all, the bear that started the line back in the twilight mists of antiquity. A bear so gigantic, it blotted out the sun with its hump. When it was thirsty, it drank whole rivers dry. When it was hungry, it ate entire herds of buffalo.

A growl from the grizzly returned Zach to the here and now, to the peril-fraught present and the imminent menace of a beast he could not possibly slay unless his father's luck was inherited.

How long had the grizzly stood there? Zach wondered. Two minutes? Five? He had lost track. That it had not attacked was encouraging. It could be the bear would leave him in peace.

Then the grizzly's upper lip curled back from its glistening sabers and it uttered an ominous growl.

Zach's gut balled into a knot. He knew what was coming as surely as night followed day and day followed night. He knew what was coming, and he did not wait for it to happen. Hauling on the reins, he wheeled the zebra dun and fled down the mountain as if all the black hounds of Hades were nipping at the dun's hoofs. A glance back confirmed the worst.

The grizzly had dropped onto all fours and was hurtling after him like a fur-clad avalanche. A roar burst from its throat, a roar that ordinarily froze its prey in place so it could dispatch them with brutal efficiency. But Zach was not ordinary prey, and the zebra dun was too panic-stricken to be paralyzed.

The thud of heavy hoofs was like the beat of drums. Or the beat of Zach's pulse in his temples. He tried not to think of how close the bear was, or the consequences if the zebra dun slipped or if he were unhorsed. He concentrated on reaching the bottom of the mountain alive. Just that and nothing more. Reach the bottom alive and by then the grizzly would be winded and he could outrun it. But life has a way of posing obstacles to the most simple of plans.

Zach came to the next section of slope and saw that it was littered with fallen trees. A storm or a chinook had felled them in droves, creating a maze difficult to negotiate at the best of times. With a grizzly after him, a single mistake or misstep spelled ruin.

Jabbing his heels against the zebra dun, Zach reined right and then reined left, cutting around fallen trees with mere inches to spare. He did not look back to see if the bear was still after him. He did not need to. He could hear it, hear the raspy wheeze of its powerful lungs, as if he were being chased by a blacksmith's bellows.

A felled pine materialized directly in the zebra dun's path. Zach reined sharply and vaulted the top of the pine where the branches were thinnest.

Again Zach reined to one side. He must not let up, must not slacken for an instant, or the bear would be on him. Boulders appeared, compounding the risk, but he made it past the first cluster.

So did the grizzly. Its raspy breaths were louder. Slowly but inevitably it was gaining. Soon the zebra dun would be within reach of the beast's claws.

Zach's mind filled with an image of Louisa. He wanted to see her again, to hold her, to experience her precious love. It was unthinkable that they would be parted. Unthinkable that she would mourn over his mortal remains—provided there were any left after the grizzly was done.

Zach gave a violent shake. Here he was, riding for his life, and he let himself be distracted! Mental discipline was called for, the kind his father always tried to impress on him. "Whether you live or die," Nate once instructed him, "can depend on keeping a level head."

More boulders materialized. Zach avoided the first one. He avoided the second. Four more formed a natural wall, so closely were they spaced. He had no time to rein around them, and they were too high for his horse to jump over. So he reined the dun toward a gap and braced for the worst.

The zebra dun raced between the two boulders with a whisker's width to spare. Once past them, Zach took a gamble and looked over his shoulder. He had to know how close the grizzly was.

The boulders slowed it, but only temporarily. Rather than try to squeeze its enormous bulk through the same gap, the grizzly, without hardly breaking stride, went up and over the boulders as if they were no real barrier at all. It slipped coming down but recovered its balance with its next bound.

Zach came to a stand of aspens and wove the zebra dun through them like a four-legged needle through a tree-trunk tapestry. He smiled, thinking that the closely spaced aspens would slow the grizzly more, but when he came to the end of the stand and glanced over his shoulder, the bear had lost only a couple yards.

The grizzly had to be tiring, Zach told himself. Over short spurts grizzlies were fast but they usually became winded much sooner than a horse. Usually.

Below the aspens were yellow pines. Maybe, Zach reflected, some of his father's luck had rubbed off on him. Yellow pines grew farther apart than aspens and spruce, and their branches were higher off the ground, resulting in more open woodland. At last he could give the zebra dun its head. He slapped his legs and whooped, his hair whipped by the wind as the zebra dun galloped flat out.

Daring another glance, Zach smiled and shouted, "You won't get me now!" But he spoke too soon.

Barely had Zach faced front than a low limb that should not be there *was* there. In pure reflex he flattened against the saddle but he was not quite quick enough; the branch struck his shoulder a jarring blow, and the next thing Zach knew, he was tumbling.

Thrusting out his free hand, Zach clung desperately to the saddle. He needed to use both hands but he had his Hawken in the other and he refused to let go. Rifles were not only costly and hard to obtain west of the Mississippi River, they were often all that stood between a frontiersman and extinction.

Zach was able to hook his right leg over the saddle but he was only delaying the inevitable. He must clamber back on or he would lose his hold and fall, and the grizzly would be on him before he could stand.

The grizzly!

A glance showed the bear had gained and was nearly nipping at the zebra dun's flanks. Zach tried to pull himself up but he could not quite get enough leverage. Tensing his shoulders, he shifted his right leg, and almost lost his grip entirely when the zebra dun came to a dip in the ground and he bounced as if he were a ball.

Something brushed his left leg. Zach thought it was a bush or a tree limb and ignored it. Then there was a tug on his pants, and twisting his head, he was appalled to see that the grizzly had nearly overtaken the zebra dun and was running almost alongside, its broad head near his trailing leg and foot. Even as he looked the bear snapped at him again, but its teeth only snagged the whangs on his buckskins. Another inch or two and those fearsome fangs would shear through flesh and bone like a sword through tallow.

The sight lent strength to Zach's limbs. Never taking his eyes off the bear, he swung onto the saddle and straightened. The grizzly bit at the zebra dun, but missed. The dun's eyes were wide with fright and it was streaking down the mountain as if its hooves were endowed with Mercury's wings, but it was not enough. The grizzly's head was now even with the zebra dun's belly. It was only a matter of seconds before the bear's teeth opened the horse like saws ripping through wood.

Zach did the only thing he could think of. He thrust the Hawken's muzzle at the bear and when it was nearly brushing the bear's eye, he fired. At that range he could not miss, under normal circumstances. But he was astride a horse moving at a frantic gallop, over uneven terrain, and just as he squeezed the trigger, a knoll loomed before them, and the zebra dun took a flying bound up it. Zach was jolted so badly that the Hawken whipped upward, and the shot intended for the grizzly's eye missed its head entirely.

The blast, though, had an unforeseen effect. It seemed to startle the monster, and it slowed drastically.

Elated, Zach gripped the reins with the same hand that held the Hawken, and drew a flintlock. The bear was pouring on speed again. He let it come almost as close as before, and fired at its head. Again he missed, but the blast of smoke and the noise brought the bear to a stop. It hit him that maybe the grizzly had never heard a gun before. He yipped for joy when it turned and started back up the mountain.

Slowing the zebra dun, Zach shoved the spent pistol under his belt, drew his other flintlock, and sent a shot in sheer spite after the brute's rapidly retreating bulk. He laughed for joy at his deliverance, kissed the pistol, and slid it back under his belt.

The zebra dun was winded and lathered with sweat but Zach could not stop. Not yet. Not until he was well in the clear. He would ride for another five minutes, then halt so the horse could rest and he could reload.

Lordy, he had been lucky. He realized more fully than ever what his father had meant. All the skill in the world could not hold a candle to plain, simple luck when a man's life hung in the balance.

Zach resisted an urge to giggle. He felt giddy with delight. He patted the zebra dun's neck but the exhausted animal barely noticed. "You did good, boy," he praised it. "Real good."

One thing was for sure, Zach reflected. He was going to have a talk with his father about Nate's plan to spare the bear by somehow training it to leave them alone. To him it had been a preposterous notion; now it was more so. That griz was a man-killer. They could no more train it not to kill them than they could train the sun to rise at a different time of the day.

Zach laughed again, this time at the silliness of it all. Train a grizzly! It was a notion worthy of a five-year-old. Of course, he would never say so to his father, but he would be damned if he would go along with it now that its futility had been rubbed in his face.

Something Shakespeare was fond of saying popped into Zach's head, another of his endless quotes from the Bard. "He has not so much brain as earwax." Zach slapped his thigh and laughed louder than ever. That fit his father's crazy idea perfectly. "He has not so much brain as earwax," he repeated aloud.

Belatedly, Zach registered the crash of underbrush to his left. A mammoth form was plowing through it like a hairy ship through a brittle sea, and almost before Zach could bring the zebra dun to a gallop, the grizzly was on top of them. Its giant maw closed with a snap, missing by a hair, and the horse exploded out of there as if a lit keg of powder had been shoved up its hind end and exploded.

Numb with disbelief, Zach was stricken by his folly. All his guns were empty. He should have reloaded as soon as he fired them. It was the first rule of survival, ingrained into him as a young boy by his father. If Nate said it once, he said it a million times; never, ever leave his guns unloaded.

Suddenly Shakespeare's quote was not nearly as hilarious.

The zebra dun swiftly pulled ahead. But it was obvious that the bear was not exerting itself to its fullest. It was content to pace them until the horse tired, then it would finish them off.

Zach's blood ran cold. Of all the ways to die, being ripped apart by a griz had to be one of the worst. It ranked up there with being burned alive at the stake. He didn't mind going down fighting. He just wanted a fair chance.

Conforming to the buck and sway of the saddle, Zach rode for his very life. They were out of the yellow pines and in a belt of mixed trees and thick brush. It slowed them. His mind screamed at him to go, go, go, but the zebra dun could only move so fast, and as tired as it was, that was not fast enough.

Zach glanced back to gauge the distance between them. The bear was loping at an easy pace, surprisingly graceful for something so enormous. "Damn you to hell," he fumed. "Why don't you find a fawn to eat?"

The blow to his chest came as a two-fold jolt: the

jolt of physical pain, and the jolt of emotional shock. Zach felt himself swept clear of the saddle, felt the Hawken go flying. Instinctively, he clutched at the limb he had struck and clung on as the zebra dun continued down the mountain.

Zach swung both legs up and wrapped them around the limb. From below came a menacing growl. He turned his head and found himself eye to eye with his pursuer. The grizzly had him. He could not possibly scramble up into the tree before it swatted him from his roost or bit him.

The bear had him and it knew it.

Zach could not say what prompted him to do what he did next. It was not spurred by a conscious thought. He just did it. He poked the grizzly in the eye just as hard as he could.

The bear reacted as a person would. It recoiled, blinking, and vented a roar of bestial resentment.

In a twinkling Zach swung on top of the branch, braced his legs, and leaped to a higher one. He did not stop there but kept climbing until he was high enough that the bear could not reach him.

The grizzly stared up balefully. The eye Zach had poked was watering, and a tear trickled down the grizzly's face.

His back to the bole, Zach shook in relief. He had come so close. He was alive, but now his horse was gone and he had lost the Hawken. He still had both pistols, though. Close up, they were powerful enough to inflict severe wounds, but he would rather not have to rely on them if he could help it. Wounded grizzlies were that much more fierce.

The grizzly rose onto its hind legs and extended a

paw as high as it could reach. Its claws were still a good ten feet short of Zach's dangling feet, and in frustration it vented another thunderous roar.

"You can't get me, you bastard," Zach gloated.

Snarling, the grizzly braced both giant forepaws against the tree, and pushed. The whole tree shook. Zach had to fling his arm around the trunk to keep from being dislodged. He was not out of danger.

The tree was a birch. A young birch, no more than thirty feet high. The upper limbs were much too slender to bear his weight, and the trunk was no thicker around than one of his mother's pie pans. An ax would cleave through it in minutes. And a bear, a really big bear with the raw strength of a hundred men, and claws and teeth as sharp as any ax, might well do the same.

Zach's skin prickled as he saw the grizzly slash at the bark. Its claws left grooves inches deep. The bear slashed again, ripping off a piece as long as Zach's forearm.

"Don't you dare, damn you."

The bear attacked the tree as if it were a rival, biting and clawing in a frenzy. Whole chunks were torn out. Zach figured it would stop soon but the grizzly bit and clawed and clawed and bit until there was a cavity six inches wide and four inches from bottom to top. Fully a third of the trunk was gone.

Zach realized that the grizzly had done this before. That it had treed prey, and had learned that the best way to bring the prey down was to bring down the tree. He climbed higher, as high as he could without the branches breaking, and set to reloading his pistols.

Suddenly the birch shook as if to a strong wind. But

it was the bear, pushing with both front paws and looking up at Zach with what Zach swore was a vicious grin.

"Go to hell," Zach said.

The bear shook harder. When that failed to dislodge Zach, the bear renewed its assault on the birch.

Zach used his teeth to open his powder horn. He carefully tilted it so the powder would dribble down the barrel. From his bullet pouch he took a bullet and a patch. "I'll fix you," he told the bear. "Just see if I don't." But he was only fooling himself. Penetrating to a grizzly's vitals was difficult under the best of circumstances. Their skulls were as thick as the armor helmets worn by knights of yore, and as impervious. Thick layers of muscle and fat protected their heart and lungs and other organs. He might as well use a pea-shooter as a .55-caliber flintlock.

The bear had stopped ripping at the trunk and was staring fixedly up at him.

"Go pester someone else," Zach said. Hearing his own voice tended to steady his frayed nerves. It reminded him that he was a man, a human being, and that what he lacked compared with the bear's vast brute strength he more than made up for with a keener intellect. There *had* to be a way to save himself. There just had to.

"Yes sir," Zach said, employing the ramrod to tamp the patch and ball down. "When my pa comes up with brainstorms, they sure are humdingers. Next he'll be wanting to throw saddles on buffalo so we can ride them."

The grizzly growled.

"My sentiments exactly," Zach said. "I don't see why

he's so upset about killing so many of your kind. Were it up to me, there wouldn't be one of you left in the whole wide world." He grinned at the colossus. "There's a thought. Maybe I should make it my life's work to wipe out every last silver-tip there is."

The grizzly snapped its jaws together, then applied them to the bôle.

"Move to a new valley, he says," Zach muttered while sliding the pistol under his belt and reaching for the other one. "It's too dangerous near the foothills, he says. Too many hostiles, he says. Too many white cut-throats coming to the mountains these days, he says." Zach turned the pistol so he could pour powder down the muzzle. "And what did I do? I said, 'Sure, Pa, whatever you want is fine by me. If you want to move, we'll move, if it means Lou is safe.'" Zach began pouring. "Safe, hell. When will I learn? There isn't any-where in these mountains where anyone is safe."

The grizzly was chewing into the birch as if it were juicy flesh.

"I learned that lesson when I was knee-high to a grasshopper," Zach rambled on. "So why is it I have to keep relearning it every few years? I feel sorry for my wife, hitching herself to a man who is as dumb as a stump." He fished another bullet and patch from his pouch.

The grizzly shook the tree.

"Come to think of it," Zach said, glancing down in anger, "maybe it's not such a bad idea, after all. You are the only griz in this valley. Once we take care of you, it will be a nice place to live."

Several inches of wood dissolved into bits and pieces.

"If I live through this," Zach informed his would-be devourer, "I don't care what my pa wants, I aim to hunt you down and treat my wife to a new rug for our cabin. How do you like that notion?"

Apparently the bear did not like it one bit. The grizzly's onslaught on the tree intensified.

"Getting hungry, are you?" Zach taunted. "Working up an appetite? Well, if worse comes to worst, I hope you choke on me, you son of a bitch." Both pistols were loaded. He aimed at the grizzly's head but he did not fire. "Only as a last resort," he said.

Zach tucked the pistols under his belt. Then, on an impulse, he unlimbered his tomahawk and chopped at a small branch above him. It was only a couple of inches thick. The tomahawk bit through in four swings. Cupping his other hand to his mouth, he yelled down, "Hey, you!" and let go of the branch.

The grizzly stopped tearing at the tree and looked up. By merest chance the branch struck it on the tip of its nose, eliciting a roar.

Cackling, Zach wagged the tomahawk. "There's more where that came from, you overgrown marmot!"

In a renewed frenzy, the grizzly tore into the birch.

Seven or eight feet above Zach was another suitable limb. Propping his legs against the bole, he slowly unfurled. It only took two swings. Holding the limb directly above the bear, he let it drop.

The subsequent roar blistered the air.

Zach chuckled. He was having fun. He would go on pelting the beast for as long as there were branches to chop off. Reaching for another, he nearly lost his footing when the birch gave a violent lurch. Had he not thrown his arm around the trunk, he would have plummeted into the grizzly's gaping maw.

"That was a close one."

The next instant there was a loud *crack*, and the entire tree tilted earthward a few degrees.

Zach glanced down. His breath caught in his throat as he realized the grizzly had clawed and chewed so much of the trunk, the birch was starting to topple. All it would take was a few pushes with the grizzly's full weight, and the tree would come crashing down.

Chapter Four

Nate King liked wielding an ax. It was hard, vigorous work, and a lot more enjoyable than, say, toting water for a bath or lugging large rocks to build a fireplace. The feel of the heavy handle as he swung, the loud thunk as the blade bit in, were a tonic for neglected muscles.

There was a trick to doing it well. A man had to establish a rhythm by swinging smoothly and precisely, and letting the ax do most of the work. The edge had to be honed as sharp as it could be, and as soon as it sank into the tree or log, it must be jerked back out with the slightest flick of the forearms, giving it no chance to become stuck.

Nate and Shakespeare had been chopping for almost an hour, felling tree after tree for their new cabins, when a hand fell urgently on Nate's shoulder from behind, and tugged. Stopping, he wiped at his sweaty brow with a sleeve as he turned.

To others the worry on Winona's face would not have been obvious, but Nate had lived with her so long, she was part of him. He could read her expressions as he could the print in a book. "What's wrong?" he immediately asked.

"Stalking Coyote," Winona used their son's Shoshone name. "He went deer hunting."

"I know."

"We just heard three shots."

"Three?" Nate was as surprised as she. Zach was an excellent shot. It invariably took him only one shot to bring down a buck or doe. Good hunters—and Nate had taught his son to be one of the best—always held their fire until they had a clear shot, and always went for the heart or the brain, or, in certain circumstances, the lungs.

"Two were pistols shots," Winona elaborated.

Nate's surprised changed to unease. It was possible, if not probable, that Zach wounded a deer and had to finish it off. But it would not take two more shots to put the animal out of its misery. One shot should suffice.

"Louisa is going up to look for him."

Nate glanced toward their camp, and sure enough, his daughter-in-law was preparing to leave. "I'll go with her."

"So will I." Shakespeare had stopped chopping and joined them.

As much as Nate would like to have his mentor along, he said, "It might be best if you stayed. Maybe we aren't the only ones here." Maybe there were hostiles about, but he did not say that. He did not need to. McNair understood.

"Off you go, then, Horatio. Don't fret on our account. We'll hunker down and keep our eyes skinned," the veteran promised.

Louisa was anxious to be off. "If you're coming, shake a leg."

Nate saddled quickly. Stepping into the stirrups, he leaned down and patted his wife's lustrous hair. "It's most likely nothing. We'll go to all this trouble, and he's perfectly fine."

"Most likely," Winona said, but her eyes urged him to hasten.

The tracks of Zach's mount were plain enough for a ten-year-old to trail. Nate kept his big bay at a trot until they came to the forest, where the dense timber forced them to go slower. The delay chafed like a too-tight belt. His natural instinct was to reach his son as fast as possible. If Zach was in dire trouble, every second counted.

As Nate rode, his mind wandered. He thought about the wilderness in which they lived, and how it was a wondrous world unto itself, a world of beauty and marvels, of majestic mountains and spectacular sunsets, of herds of buffalo a million strong, of mountain sheep poised precariously over a precipice. But she was a harsh mistress, this wilderness. She never forgave a mistake. Commit one, and a man might not live to see the next dawn.

It took some getting used to.

When Nate first came to the Rockies, the relentless violence shocked and sickened him. He had wanted no part of the endless taking of life.

Kill or be killed was the unwritten law of the wilds. Every animal killed something else to survive. Big insects ate little insects. Birds and small mammals ate both. Snakes and lizards ate whatever they could catch. Hawks and eagles and owls preyed on snakes and lizards and small mammals. Then there were the bigger predators: the bobcats, lynx, cougars, and bears.

Even those animals that did not eat meat killed other things. Beaver killed trees to make their dams. Rabbits and other plant-eaters killed the plants they consumed.

Over and over, on and on, the cycle was repeated. Killing in order to keep breathing. Taking life in order to live. It was the natural way of things, and branded as a bald-faced lie humankind's greatest accomplishment.

Civilization was not natural. Civilization was an attempt by humanity to deny the natural order by breaking the cycle of kill or be killed so that human beings could live in relative peace and security. Civilization pampered and coddled and fostered the illusion that the real world was a much nicer and safer place than it really was. Civilization was an exercise in self-delusion.

Most people did not realize it. Most thought that civilized values were the values of the natural world. They imposed their delusions on the creatures that lived in the wild, compounding their folly. Bears were regarded as cute and cuddly. Cats that brought mice and birds into a house were smacked and scolded for being mean and bad. Eagles were made into national symbols.

The human race never lacked for silliness. Nowhere was that more apparent than in their constant desire to remold the natural world in the fashion they wanted it to be instead of adapting to the natural order of things.

Nate was one of the relative few who would rather adapt than delude himself. He recognized the world for what it was, and lived accordingly. It had been a bitter lesson, learned at the expense of his uncle's life and many others he cared about. A lesson so ingrained, it molded his thoughts and his actions without him consciously realizing that it did.

Now, pushing the bay as fast as the terrain permitted, Nate remembered those he had lost, and the lesson learned, and in his heart of hearts grew a secret fear that only the sight of his son could quell.

To "live in dread" was once a common figure of speech. Back when humans had to slay their own food or starve, each hunt was one from which the hunters might not return.

Civilization changed that. Civilization protected and pampered those who lived under its umbrella. When people's needs were handed to them on a monetary platter, when all they had to do was plunk down money to eat and drink and put clothes on their backs, the natural order was blunted.

Nate believed that most people preferred things that way. They would rather be protected from life than experience life as it really was. They did not seem to mind that the safety they craved came at a great cost. They did not seem to care that in exchange for keeping nature at bay, they must give up their freedom.

To live truly free was a state few ever attained. For most, their conduct was dictated by laws and rules and custom. Their every waking moment was spent conforming to how others wanted them to live rather than living as they wanted.

Civilization was of great benefit in some regards. It bestowed a degree of safety and ease of living, but what it demanded in return was a treasure beyond compare. Only when a man or woman had tasted a truly free life could they recognize the limits civilization imposed, and recognize those limits for what they really were: a prison, a form of captivity, a cage made not of iron or steel bars but of society's constraints.

Nate would rather be free. He would rather live with the daily dread than spend each day with a leash around his neck. There was a rich tapestry to life available only to those who shattered civilization's shackles and dared to relate to reality on its own terms.

A sudden question from Louisa brought Nate out of himself. "Do you hear that? What is it? It's coming our way."

Something was crashing down the mountain toward them.

Nate drew rein and brought his Hawken to his shoulder. Whatever was approaching, he would be ready. He rested his thumb on the hammer. Every nerve tingling, he distinguished a large shape plowing through the undergrowth like a bull gone amok.

His first thought was that it must be a bear. Bears were notorious for flattening everything in their path when their dander was up. And if it was a bear, then it must be the grizzly he had encountered on his last visit.

Suddenly the three shots made sense. Fear spiked through Nate, fear that his oldest had met the fate that by rights should have been his. Zach had run into the grizzly and it had killed him. Now the griz was after more flesh to devour.

"And I was going to spare you," Nate said softly while aligning the Hawken's sights. He saw now why everyone had been so dead-set against the idea. They did not want to end up as Zach had.

Then the underbrush parted and out of it galloped the zebra dun, its mane flying, lathered with sweat from its neck to its hindquarters.

"It's Zach's horse!" Louisa cried, goading hers to intercept it. "What could have happened?"

Nate was still partial to his bear idea. The grizzly had done what the Blackfeet, Bloods and Piegans never could. His hunch was reinforced when they brought the zebra dun to a halt and he found long gashes in its flank.

"Are those claw marks?" Louisa had gone as pale as a sheet.

"You stay with the dun," Nate said. "I'll backtrack."

"Not on your life," Louisa responded. "Zach is my husband, remember? I have as much of a stake as you do." Swinging lithely down, she hurriedly wrapped the zebra dun's reins around a tree limb, then climbed back on. "What are we waiting for?"

The panicked zebra dun had left a swath of crushed vegetation in its wake. Nate applied his heels to the bay. He climbed rapidly, half expecting at any moment to come around a tree and find the mangled body of his oldest.

Louisa was as grim as death. She soon caught up with the bay, then passed it. Nate was going to suggest she stay behind him in case they ran into the grizzly, but he changed his mind. She would refuse, and there was no arguing with a woman when the one she loved was in peril. Winona had taught him that.

The trees thinned. In the distance rose a high ridge. Beyond the ridge were snow-capped peaks. To the northwest the glacier was an emerald green gem against a backdrop of white. The highest peaks were to the southwest. Beyond them lay impenetrable mystery, impenetrable in the sense that no white man had ever crossed them. White eyes had never beheld whatever lay on the other side.

There was a time when the very thought would set Nate's pulse quickening. He had relished exploring new country, relished the sense of adventure that came with being the first white man to venture into unknown territory. Somewhere or other he had lost that sense of adventure. A family to tend for was part of the reason. In his opinion, to rear a family proper a man had to set down roots. A home and a stable life took precedence over gallivanting all over creation. But now that Zach was married and Evelyn old enough to help her mother look after the cabin, Nate had begun to feel that familiar twinge. The urge to see what lay over those peaks. The urge to once again go where no white man had gone before.

A yell from Louisa bought Nate back to the here and now. She was pointing at something higher up.

It took a few seconds for Nate to make sense of what he was seeing. A birch tree had fallen against several pines, and under it, plainly visible on the ground, lay a torn buckskin shirt.

"Good God. Is that Zach's?"

Now it was Nate who passed Louisa. He sprang

from the saddle before the bay came to a stop and sank to his knees next to the shirt. Teeth and claws had shredded it like so much paper. And now that he had a better look at the birch, Nate saw where teeth and claws had done the same to the trunk.

Louisa was at his elbow. "It is his, isn't it?"

"Yes." Nate was wearing one exactly like it. Both bore the unmistakable stamp of Winona's craftsmanship in the style of the beadwork, and the fact that she only ever used blue beads, her favorite.

"Then where is Zach?" Louisa asked, gazing anxiously around. "He has to be here somewhere."

Nate wished he knew.

For Zachary King, the moment when the tree started to fall was one of the most harrowing of his life. Waiting below, intent on ripping him apart and dining on the pieces, was the monstrous grizzly. It actually seemed to grin as it pressed against the birch with all its might.

There was a loud *crack*.

"Do your worst, you hairy bastard," Zach fumed. He still had his pistols but he would only use them if left no recourse. The tomahawk was in his right hand, his left was wrapped around a branch.

The birch dipped another foot or so, then stopped.

Thwarted, the grizzly roared. It chewed at the bole but the tree would not fall lower.

Zach laughed and smacked the birch in relief. He hoped the bear would give up. He wanted nothing so much as to see it hindquarters receding in the distance.

The grizzly continued to tear at the soft wood. Soon the birch tilted another foot or so toward the earth.

Zach licked his lips and braced for the worst. Any moment now the tree would crash down, the grizzly would pounce, and what little was left of his body after the grizzly was done would lie in mute testimony to the senselessness of his end.

"Not if I can help it," Zach said. Sliding the tomahawk's haft under his belt, he removed his powderhorn, ammo pouch and possibles bag, and hung them over a limb by their straps. Then he hastily pried at his buckskin shirt. Once it was off, he balled it up and held it in his right hand.

The griz was a flesh-and-blood buzzsaw, determined to topple the tree no matter how long it took. Mere wood could not withstand the onslaught much longer.

Again the birch gave a jolt, nearly spilling Zach, and with a sustained crack, eased earthward as slowly as a falling feather. Instantly, the bear ran directly under Zach and rose onto its hind legs.

"Eat this!" Zach cried, and threw his shirt at the grizzly's head. He meant to confuse it for the few seconds it would take to leap to the ground and bolt for his life, but his aim was better than he dared hope, and the effect remarkable. For the bottom billowed as the shirt dropped, like a pillow case if swung real hard, and the open end slipped neatly over the bear's muzzle and eyes, much like a glove fits over a hand.

For a few seconds the grizzly was transfixed in bestial astonishment. Then it clawed at the shirt in a firestorm of primal rage.

At the same instant, the birch came to a stop. Several pines had stopped its descent, leaving Zach suspended a good fifteen feet in the air. He might be just out of the bear's reach, or he might not. He did not care to wait around to find out. Coiling his legs, he sprang clear and landed hard on his heels less than six feet from the carnivore.

One eye was clear of the shirt and it fixed on Zach with burning intensity.

Zach fled. He could not hope to outrun the beast but he could find another tree to climb, one with a thicker trunk this time, or possibly a hiding place, although the grizzly's exceptional sense of smell would ferret him out unless the hiding place was equally exceptional.

He had lost his bearings while in the birch, but now Zach saw by the sun that he was heading west. Pines lent the illusion of shelter but they were no more protection than twigs would be. Racing headlong through them, he desperately searched for a safe haven. But there was none. Just more pines and more brush and an occasional boulder.

"Damn it," Zach snarled, and was answered by another growl, much louder, from somewhere to his rear.

The grizzly was after him.

Zach had never thought of himself as particularly religious. If pressed, he would admit he was more partial to his mother's beliefs than his father's. But now he prayed as he had seldom ever done, prayed that the Almighty or the Great Mystery or however it was known would see fit to spare him. He did not want to die. He had too much living to do. Years of sharing a warm bed with Lou, of maybe having kids and a family and being the kind of father to them that his own father had been to him.

The thought jarred him. Zach had never considered that part of married life. Louisa was forever going on about how she wanted children some day, but he took her prattling as a matter of womanly course.

Loud sniffing told him the grizzly had lost sight of him and was following him by scent. He avoided brushing against the vegetation he passed but that would not be enough; his scent would hang in the air, invisible but there for the griz to detect and point the way as surely as a painted sign.

To make Zach's life-or-death predicament worse, the trees were thinning out. Soon the bear would spot him and pour on a burst of speed.

As if to seal Zach's fate, the slope angled upward more steeply than ever. Bending at the waist, he used his hands for extra purchase. Scrambling like an oversized crab, he kicked loose pebbles from under his flying moccasins.

Then there were no trees at all. Zach plunged through a thicket and took a long stride past it, and had to throw out his arms to preserve his balance as his right foot flailed empty air. Startled, he glanced down. His breath was taken away by the sheer precipice he had nearly plunged over, a cliff two hundred feet high, with jagged boulders at the bottom.

Stepping back from the edge, Zach dropped to his knees. That had been much too close, but then, so had being treed by the grizzly. *The grizzly!* He heard it sniff about a dozen yards behind him. A breeze blowing over the cliff had confused it. Most of Zach's scent had been borne off, and the bear was trying to figure out which way he had gone.

Hope flared anew, but Zach was only fooling himself. The griz would find him. It was inevitable. He could go north or south along the cliff rim and try to circle back but it would only delay the end result. It would be better if he could lose the grizzly entirely.

To that end, Zach peered over the edge. Eight feet below, growing out of the cliff face, was a stunted tree. How it took root there, he could not begin to guess. Plant life had a knack for thriving in the most inhospitable of places. Maybe a seed had been blown into a crack. The important thing was that the tree was there, and offered a promise of salvation.

Zach studied the stone surface between the edge and the tree. Although it appeared smooth, it wasn't. A network of cracks and protrusions suggested a means of carrying out his plan. Part of him balked, though. One slip, the slightest miscalculation, and he would plummet to a horrible death below.

A growl from the bear warned Zach his enemy was closer.

Taking a deep breath, Zach swung his legs over the edge and carefully lowered them until the toes of his right foot found a crack. It was tenuous but bore his weight. He eased his left hand to a knob and wrapped his fingers so tight, his knuckles were white.

The thicket rustled. There was a loud grunt.

It would not be long, Zach realized. He lowered his other leg, located a suitable grip for his other hand. He shut his mind to the dizzying height, and to the fact he was clinging to sheer rock like a buckskin-clad lizard. Swallowing hard, he inched lower, probing with his toes. His head slipped below the rim. His cheek and the skin of his bare chest scraped stone.

With consummate care Zach extended his leg as far

as it would go. His sole made contact with the tree. He shifted his leg to better distribute his weight, then cautiously lowered his other leg.

A sudden strong gust buffeted him. Instinctively, Zach clutched at the cliff with all his might. His legs started to shake but he stilled them by force of will. He would not give in to panic. He would not let fear take over. He would do what he had to in order to survive.

Another gust fanned him, from above. A gust of fetid air that was not the breeze but something else entirely.

Zach looked up.

The giant bulk of the grizzly loomed huge against the stark blue of the sky. Its claws framed the rim, its legs were as thick as redwoods, its massive head blotted out the sun. From deep in its chest came a long, low rumble.

Damn you, Zach was tempted to shout, but did not. His plan had gone awry. He had not counted on this. He figured the bear would sniff about awhile up top, then leave. Now that it knew where he was, it could easily wait him out. Eventually hunger and thirst would compel him to climb back up, and the grizzly would have its meal.

But the grizzly was not disposed to wait. Abruptly sinking onto its belly, it thrust out a paw. Claws lightly brushed Zach's hair but the bear could not quite reach him.

Zach debated whether to draw his pistol and shoot the bear in the head. He elected not to for two reasons. First, it might merely make the bear mad and goad it into something rash and mutually fatal. Second, the smoke would get into his eyes and nose, and blurry vision or a fit of coughing were the last things he needed.

The grizzly was trying to ease lower. Again it swung an enormous paw, and Zach ducked. Bearing its teeth, it growled in annoyance.

"You will have to do better than that."

The bear took his advice to heart. It wriggled its bulk until its head and shoulders were below the edge. But it had to keep one front paw braced on the rim, and that limited its reach with the other. Twice it raked its claws and twice raked air because its quarry crouched low.

Zach could not help himself; he laughed. The bear's bafflement was comical. But it would not stay baffled long. Sooner or later it would dawn on the grizzly to brace its right paw against the cliff face itself, and it would be all over except the bleeding and the fall and the searing agony of having every bone in his body shattered to bits and his flesh reduced to unrecognizable pulp.

They locked eyes.

"I hope my death teaches my pa a lesson," Zach said. "I just wish I could be there when he kills you." He was talking to bolster his confidence but it did not work. He always had a pragmatic nature, and it would not do to deceive himself when he was literally staring death in its hairy face.

The grizzly slid its other paw over the edge to a niche that could support it, opened its maw wide, and roared.

Zach's end was nigh.

Chapter Five

A parent's love is the strongest love there is. A spouse's love did not always stay true, but the love of a devoted parent for a child was a bond that could not be broken this side of the grave.

So when Nate King heard the grizzly's fearsome roar, his love for his son caused him to do that which he would not normally do. Heedless of the risk, he recklessly whipped the bay into a gallop and charged up the slope. All he could think of was that his son was in danger.

Louisa was ten yards behind.

The bear heard the thunder of hoofs and reared to confront them.

Reining up, Nate fixed a hasty bead on the grizzly's throat. He had a clear shot. All he had to do was stroke the trigger. But he could not bring himself to do it. "Zach? Are you all right?" he hollered, and was answered with a holler from somewhere past the grizzly.

"I'm not hurt, Pa! But I need help."

Nate fired into the air.

Whether it was the blast or the sudden advent of Louisa on her mount that caused the monster to drop onto all fours and retreat to the north, Nate would never know. The bear was barely out of sight when he was off the bay and dashing to the cliff rim. His heart hammering, he peered down. "It didn't get you?" His voice broke, and he could not say more for the constriction in his throat.

"Is the griz dead?" Zach eagerly asked.

Nate did not answer the question. Instead he urged, "Hold on! I'll have you off of there in two shakes of a raven's tail feathers."

"There's no hurry, Pa." Zach grinned. "I'm not going anywhere."

But Nate did hurry. He envisioned his son slipping, and the consequences, and he snatched his rope from the parfleche in which he kept it coiled, and dashed back to the edge, unraveling the rope as he went so all he had to do was snake it over the rim so it fell within Zach's easy grasp. "Give me one more second," Nate called down, and wrapped the other end around his middle.

By then Lou was next to him, relief fighting with horror on her face. "Zachary! Don't move!"

"Darn. I was going to hop up and down a few times for the fun of it."

Nate set himself and gripped the rope in both hands. Lou added her hands without being asked. "Ready when you are, son!"

Even though they were braced, Zach's weight caused them to dig in their heels and grit their teeth. Lou closed her eyes and leaned back, straining with all her strength.

"Lordy, he's heavy."

Nate grunted in agreement. His boy was solid muscle. The rope dug into his palms and fingers and his arms bulged like corded steel. Locking his knees, he refused to be budged until his son was safe.

Zach's right hand appeared, groping for a hold, then his left. He pulled himself over the rim and lay with half his body on top and half dangling. Red in the face, he smiled. But his smile faded when he glanced to either side and noticed something conspicuous by its absence. "I thought you shot the damn griz?'

"I scared it off," Nate confessed.

"You what?" Zach was on his knees, and he was none too happy. "That bear came near to making worm food of me, and you let it live?"

"I told you before," Nate said, relaxing his arms. "I don't want to kill it if I can help it."

Louisa sprang to Zach and warmly threw her arms around him. "Thank heaven you're safe! I've been worried sick since we found your horse."

Zach was too mad to acknowledge her. Glaring at his father, he said, "Maybe you don't understand, Pa. That griz chased me down and damn near mauled me. I barely made it into a tree. But that didn't stop that bear. No sir. It chewed through half the trunk and would have done the same to me, but I was lucky and got away." He gestured sharply at the cliff. "Only to wind up here, no better off than when I was in the tree." His voice rose. "I want that damn bear dead. Do you hear me? I want it as dead as dead can be."

"We'll talk about this more after you have calmed down some," Nate proposed as he coiled his rope.

"Calmed down?" Zach exploded. "Have you heard a word I just said? None of us are safe so long as that critter is breathing. Either you do what needs doing, or so help me, I will."

"I don't want the bear touched if we can help it," Nate said.

Zach walked up and did something he had never done before in his entire life. He poked his father in the chest. "Give me one good reason! Just one! And it had better be a good one."

"That grizzly saved my life."

"What?" both Zach and Louisa blurted at the same time, with Zach demanding, "What in blazes are you talking about?"

Nate stared at peeled skin on his palms. His hands stung like the dickens, but the sting was nothing compared with the hurt he felt inside. "Do you remember Rabid Wolf?" he asked. "The young Ute who hated whites?"

"How could we forget him?" Zach rejoined. "He raided our cabins, destroyed most of our possessions, and came within a whisker of rubbing you out."

Nodding, Nate turned and hung the rope from his saddle. "He followed me here the first time I came. Him and three of his friends. They had it in for me, but I dealt with his friends."

"You never told us what happened to Rabid Wolf," Louisa mentioned. "Only that he was dead."

"Rabid Wolf outfoxed me," Nate revealed. "He had me at his mercy, and he was about to bury his tomahawk in my face when that grizzly you want me to kill came up behind him and separated his arm from his body. Then it dragged him off to eat." He paused. "You can see why I don't want to kill it, can't you?"

"That griz could just as well have killed you as Rabid Wolf. It wasn't saving your hide. It was hungry, and the Ute was handy."

"It still saved me," Nate said.

"I don't believe you, Pa. I truly don't." Zach shook his head in dismay. "You're missing the most important point. That griz has had a taste of human flesh, and you know as well as I do that once a bear eats a human, it's liable to come back for a second and third helping."

"That's a good point," Louisa inserted.

Frowning, Nate leaned on the saddle. "Not if we can teach it to leave us be. Not if we can train it just like we would train a dog or a horse."

"Here you go again, babbling nonsense," Zach snapped. "Remember that fella in St. Louis who had the animal act? Professor something-or-other?"

"Peabody," Nate said.

"Yeah. Him. He had a trained bear, as I recollect. And right up there on stage he told us that bears are harder to train than any animal alive. They are as unpredictable as sin, and will as soon bite the hand that feeds them as do a trick. Do you remember?"

"Yes."

"Professor Peabody was talking about black bears. And so what if a few of them have been taught a few things? You're talking about a *grizzly*." Zach put his hands on his hips. "Has anyone in the entire history of the human race ever tamed a griz, that you know of?"

"Just because it hasn't been done before doesn't mean it can't be."

"What was that word you always used when we were little and griped about doing chores?" Zach snapped his fingers. "Nitpicking. That was it. Well, you are nitpicking now."

"Is it too much to ask that you let me try?"

Zach nodded at the cliff. "Do I really need to answer? We are none of us safe so long as that bear is breathing." He walked past his father toward his wife's horse. "Take me down the mountain, hon, before I say something I might regret."

Louisa gestured in helpless sympathy to Nate, then hurried to do as Zach wished. He waited until she climbed on, then he swung up behind her and wrapped an arm around her waist.

"As soon as I can, I am going out after your savior," Zach announced. "It's me or him, Pa. You can stop me if you want, but if you do, Lou and I will find somewhere else to live. So help me."

In all their years together, Nate had never seen his son so mad at him. He wanted to say more but Lou wheeled her mount and the pair were soon lost to view. Discouraged, Nate stepped to the edge of the cliff, and sighed. Before him spread a sprawling vista of tall timber and taller peaks but he was not in any frame of mind to appreciate the scenic wonders.

Was he being foolish? Nate asked himself. Was he letting false sentiment color his judgment? Was the end result worth the worry to his family? Was it worth the loss of his son's respect?

Nate climbed on the bay and drifted toward the lake. He was in no great hurry. Zach and Winona were bound to take him to task. Perhaps Shakespeare, too. He would get there when he got there.

Absorbed in thought, Nate had descended half a mile when he spied a rider waiting for him in a clearing ahead. To say he was surprised was an understatement. "Does your mother know you are up here?"

"I left when she wasn't paying attention," Evelyn admitted, adding defensively, "She didn't say I couldn't go riding."

"You followed us all this way?" Nate marveled. "Didn't it dawn on you how dangerous that was?"

"You were easy to trail, Pa," Evelyn said, "and you were in such a hurry, you never looked back. Louisa neither." She smiled a tentative smile. "Please don't be mad. I'm not stupid. I always kept you in sight, and was ready to yell if I needed you. Plus I had my artillery." She patted her rifle and the pair of pistols wedged under her belt. "I never go anywhere without them, just like you taught me."

"Nice try. But you broke our rules, and your mother and I will decide how to deal with you later."

"That's hardly fair," Evelyn objected. "I was worried about Zach. How can you hold that against me?"

Nate reined up next to her. "Right is right and wrong is wrong and what you did is wrong. It could have gotten you killed. There's a grizzly on the prowl, and it is none too friendly."

"So Zach told me," Evelyn revealed. "He also said something about you owing your life to this griz. How can that be?"

Once more Nate explained. He figured his daughter would be more understanding than his hotheaded son, but he figured wrong.

"It wasn't the grizzly saved you from Rabid Wolf. It was Providence."

"There is more to it." Nate was sorry he ever mentioned his plan. Better to keep his mouth shut and spare himself the aggravation. He gigged the bay.

"I know," Evelyn said, wheeling her mare and bringing it into step alongside. "You are sick and tired of killing bears. You want to declare a truce. But a white flag doesn't mean a thing to a griz."

"I would rather not talk about it," Nate said. Nothing he could say would persuade any of them.

"That's not the pa I grew up with," Evelyn said. "He would never tuck tail, whether with words or in a fight. When he had something to do he went out and did it, and anyone who stood in his way was tromped under."

Nate chuckled. "I couldn't hardly tromp on my own wife and children, now could I?"

"You never were a hitter like some fathers I've heard about," Evelyn said lightheartedly, "and for that I was glad. A good tongue-lashing now and again was the worst you ever did."

"None of which has anything to do with the grizzly," Nate observed.

"Sure it does. Ma never hit us because Shoshones don't believe in beating their kids. You never beat us, either, but not because of the Shoshones. Your pa beat you a lot when you were growing up, and because of that, you never laid a finger on us. You did not want us to go through what you went through."

"Your point?"

"I trust you to do what is best for us. I don't much like the notion of having a grizzly around but if you think it will be all right, I'll go along with whatever you want." Evelyn beamed. "Because I love you, too."

Nate had never wanted to hug her as much as he did right that moment. Yet, in the wellspring of his being, he was deeply troubled. He could not guarantee that everything would be all right. He could not beyond all shadow of doubt state with certainty that the grizzly would never try to harm them.

"So how exactly do we go about teaching a bear to fight shy of us?" Evelyn inquired.

"I haven't quite worked that out yet."

"We could chase it over into the next range," Evelyn proposed. "That way we could live in peace."

"We could try, yes," Nate said. But herding a grizzly was not like herding a cow. Cows did not have nasty tempers and teeth and claws that could rend and slay. "Although what is to stop it from coming back?"

"Maybe if we drove it far enough away?"

"A hundred miles? Two hundred?" Nate shook his head. "We would have to drive it clear to California."

"You'll think of something," Evelyn said with confidence. "You always do."

Nate contrasted his daughter's complete faith in him with his son's complete lack. "There's a lot at stake."

"Isn't there always?" Evelyn retorted. "Hardly a month goes by that one of us doesn't come close to meeting our Maker."

"That will change once we have settled in and the grizzly is dealt with," Nate said. But would it? Or was he deceiving himself? He shook his head, refusing to dwell on it any longer. All this thinking was giving him a headache. "Despite the griz, do you like it here?" he changed the subject.

"It's as pretty as can be," Evelyn said without much enthusiasm. "But it's not St. Louis or New Orleans."

"You still want to go live east of the Mississippi?" Nate asked. "After all you went through the last time you were there?"

Evelyn shrugged. "The white world isn't heaven, like I once believed. But for all its flaws, it has a lot to offer."

"Such as?"

"No grizzlies. No hostiles. No rattlesnakes coiled by the corral when I go to feed my horse. No wolves howling outside my window at night. No mountain lions waking me up with their screams."

Nate sighed. She had recited the same complaints many times. "I thought you were over your hatred of the wilderness?"

"I don't hate it, exactly," Evelyn said. "St. Louis doesn't have mountains that touch the sky. New Orleans doesn't have sunsets half as beautiful. Uncle Shakespeare says it's not where we live, it's what we make of where we live." She fluttered her lips. "I haven't made up my mind yet whether I'll stay or go."

"I won't pressure you," Nate said, but in his heart of hearts he dearly wanted her to stay.

On that accord they rode in silence for a spell, until Nate happened to glance down and see tracks that set off a warning peal. "Hold up." Dismounting, he hunkered and ran his fingers over one of the clearest.

"What are those? The look like big ferret prints."

"Ferrets are never this high up," Nate said. "These were made by a glutton."

"A what?"

"A wolverine," Nate clarified. An extremely large wolverine. Its front tracks were seven inches long. The average was between four and five. Yet another potential peril his family must be on the alert against.

The new valley lost more of its appeal. Convincing the grizzly to leave them alone would be difficult enough. Convincing a wolverine was impossible. Unbelievably savage, they lived to kill. Although smaller than grizzlies and mountain lions, they were known to bring down full-grown moose. Nate once witnessed a clash between a wolverine and a cougar over a deer the cougar had slain, and it was the wolverine that drove the cougar off. The Shoshones had many tales of wolverine ferocity, and considered seeing a wolverine, or its tracks, bad medicine.

Suddenly feeling tired beyond his years, Nate forked leather, and sighed.

Ever sensitive to those around her, Evelyn asked, "What's wrong, Pa?"

"Nothing."

"Didn't you always tell us never to lie to one another? Something is the matter, and I'm a good listener."

"You are the best daughter any man could have," Nate said. Through a gap in the pines the lake was visible, shimmering like a blue-green jewel.

She would not let it drop. "Then what?"

"I'm having second thoughts. Maybe coming here wasn't such a great notion. Maybe we should have stayed where we were."

"You're worried, aren't you? That this valley is a lot more dangerous than the other one?"

"I drove off or killed all the meat eaters from the other one," Nate said. "You could go for a walk any time of the day or night and be fairly safe."

"Fairly," Evelyn repeated. "But there were always hostiles and renegades to watch out for. And we never knew when a bear or mountain lion might wander through." She smiled up at him. "I wouldn't exactly call it tame."

Across the valley a large bird soared with outstretched wings on updrafts. Nate thought it was a hawk until he looked closer; evidently they shared the new valley with a golden eagle.

Evelyn gazed in the direction he was staring. "Should I worry about that, too? About it swooping down and carrying me off like that big eagle in Europe you read about? Or should I fret about falling into a den of rattlesnakes? Or being attacked by a herd of rabbits?"

Despite himself, Nate laughed. "Since when do rabbits attack people? You're being ridiculous."

"I'm not the only one. We can't spend our days worrying about every little thing that can go wrong or we won't get any living done."

Once again Nate was reminded that his little pride and joy was not so little anymore. On the cusp of womanhood, she was mature beyond her years. Hardship had a way of doing that.

"Anyway, this is nothing compared to the old days. Blue Water Woman and Ma were telling me about the monsters and other things that used to roam the world. Didn't the Indians believe in a bird ten times as big as an eagle? So big, it could carry off a buffalo calf?"

"Thunderbirds, they were called," Nate said. "A Shoshone elder told me that once a year the thunderbirds came from far to the south about the same time the buffalo were calving. They would stay about a month, then fly south again. The whole while, the Shoshones were afraid to step out of their lodges."

"I would be too," Evelyn said. "And how about the dwarves with their tiny poison arrows? And those hairy creatures you ran into years ago, before I was born? What were they again?"

"I never knew," Nate said. It happened when Zach was three years old. Nate had gone off with others to trap in an unexplored valley rich with beaver, and encountered creatures the Crows called Mountain Devils. Hairy things, standing eight feet tall, some of them, with conical heads and no necks to speak of. Things that slew everyone else in his party. By the grace of God he made it out, but to this day he occasionally had nightmares about snarling hulks that attacked in the black of night and ripped people apart.

"Thank goodness there aren't any of them here. Or any of the hairy elephants the Indians say used to roam these parts. And those big cats with teeth as long as Bowie knives."

"You're saying it could be a lot worse?" Nate said. "That I should be thankful all we have to worry about are a grizzly and wolverine and a mountain lion or two?"

"I'm saying I won't worry if you don't. I'll miss our old cabin, sure, but I can be as happy here as anywhere else. Happier, maybe, since we'll be closer to Zach and Uncle Shakespeare."

That was something, Nate supposed. Still, a father could not help feeling anxious when there was cause to be, and he had more cause than a father in, say, New York City or New Orleans.

After a bit Evelyn asked, "Do you think there really were all those creatures the Indians say there were?"

"The Indians should know. They were here long before the white man. Some tribes pass their history down by word of mouth. Others keep a record of events on hides and such." Nate paused. "When I was out to Oregon Country, I ran into a tribe that would not go near a certain lake. It was in the crater of an old volcano, and the Indians claimed that at one time it was home to creatures that sounded an awful lot to me like giant lobsters or crayfish."

Evelyn giggled. "Now those I would like to see."

"No, you wouldn't. The Indians say the lobsters attacked anyone who went near the lake, and couldn't be killed with arrows or lances."

"At least we don't have any of those critters hereabouts," Evelyn remarked. "So cheer up, Pa. We'll make do here as we have always made do. Things will work out. You'll see."

Nate thought to himself: Shouldn't he be the one telling her that? He only hoped she was right, and that he wasn't making the worst mistake of his life. He had enough regrets. Losing someone he loved because he was being pigheaded was not one he cared to add to the list.

Chapter Six

First things first.

Nate's attempt to teach the monarch of the valley the errors of its ursine ways had to wait until after the cabins were built. Since he was the one who had uprooted everyone, he felt he owed it to them to put a roof over their heads before doing anything else. Consequently, along with Shakespeare and Zach, he spent week after long, grueling week chopping and sawing and hewing and constructing.

They flipped a coin. Zach won the toss so they built Zach and Louisa's cabin first. As soon as it was completed, the women and Evelyn moved in. Then the men set to work on Shakespeare's cabin.

It was the same routine daily: up at dawn, have coffee and breakfast, work until noon, take half an hour to eat and relax, then more hours of hard toil until the sun dipped to the Western horizon. Often, they went back to work after supper, working by lantern light until their eyelids were heavy and their arms leaden.

Nate took on the lion's share of the labor. He often skipped the midday meal and wolfed his supper so he could work that much longer.

Winona tried to get him to stop pushing so hard, but she had the impression everything she said went in one ear and bounced out. Near the sixth week she walked up to him one evening as he was trimming a beam to use as a rafter and watched him awhile before saying, "You did not eat supper."

"I'm not hungry."

"You have to be. You have been working since sunrise. I saved some venison and bread, and I made a new pot of coffee."

Nate did not look up from the log. "You are a daisy. But I'll eat after I stop for the night."

"And when will that be? Midnight? Zach and Shakespeare stopped at sunset. You should have done the same." Winona affectionately placed a hand on his arm. "Please. For me. You are working yourself to death, and for no reason."

"Wrong. I have plenty of reasons. And you are one of them." Nate set down the plane. Arching his spine, he pressed a hand to his lower back, and grimaced. "I'm not as young and spry as I used to be."

"Spry enough for me," Winona grinned. She ran a finger across his chin and plucked at his beard. "Now come. I will not take no for an answer."

"Women," Nate said.

"Men," Winona retorted, and clasped his big hand in her small one. "As for using me as an excuse, I am perfectly content to wait for my cabin a few extra weeks if it means you will eat as you should and get more than five hours sleep a night."

"I applaud your patience," Nate said, "but I'll keep on as I have been until Evelyn and you have your new home."

"You are too stubborn, husband."

"Takes ones to know one," Nate grinned.

"Is it me," Winona asked, still serious, "or do you suffer from an excess of guilt these days?"

They were heading toward the campfire. To the north, across the lake, a lamp glowed in the window of Zach's cabin. On the south shore, Shakespeare's cabin was nearly done. All that remained was to hang the door and finish a counter.

"Ours is next," Nate said. "By the end of the month at the latest, you and Evelyn will be sleeping in beds with a roof over your heads."

Above them a myriad of stars sparkled. The night sky never failed to fill Nate with breathless wonder at the immensity of it all. A stiff wind stirred the cottonwoods and willows. To the northwest, from somewhere near the glacier, a wolf voiced the eerie, lonesome howl of its breed, a howl that wavered across the valley. Deep in the woods an owl hooted, and out in the lake something made a loud splash.

"It is magnificent here," Winona remarked. "I am glad you brought us."

"Tell me that again a year from now."

"What will be different then?" Winona inquired, and intuitively divined the answer. "Oh. If we are still alive, you mean? Goodness, you can be morbid."

"I don't even know what the word means," Nate fibbed. "You must read my dictionary in your spare time." He snapped his fingers. "I fogot. My dictionary was destroyed with the rest of my books. Damn Rabid Wolf to hell."

"We will replace your books," Winona promised. "Haven't we already ordered those you like most from the trader at Bent's Fort?"

"And they'll only take six months to get here," Nate griped. He missed his library more than anything, missed sitting in front of the fireplace in the evening and feeding his mind the best literature had to offer.

Nate regarded reading as a tonic for the soul. As a boy he spent many hours giving wing to his imagination through the stories he read. He had particularly liked to read about men who braved the frontier, men who became legends, the likes of Jim Bowie, Davy Crockett and Daniel Boone.

Bowie had been Nate's favorite. Now there was a man! Totally fearless, a wizard with the blade that bore his name, Jim Bowie cut a wide swath through the bayou country and most of Texas, and would have died a rich man had he not elected to take part in the famous stand at the Alamo.

Only later had Nate learned that Bowie once dabbled in the slave trade. Nate did not believe in the practice, himself. On moral grounds he considered it wrong for one human being to lord it over another. But the custom was widespread, and not just in the United States.

"A kiss for your thoughts, husband," Winona pried.

"I was admiring the night," Nate fibbed. She was not as fond of Bowie as he was. The slavery issue, the land swindles, Bowie's search for a lost silver mine, to Winona they smacked of greed and low character. She did not understand that a man measured his success by how well he provided for his loved ones.

"It is nice that we have each picked sites on opposite shores of the lake," Winona commented. "We are close, but not too close. I can walk to Blue Water Woman's and Louisa's cabins whenever I want to have a cup of tea with them, or borrow some sugar."

"You become more white all the time," Nate teased.

Winona blinked. "I will take that as a compliment. Just as you should accept my compliment about how hard you work, and do as I ask and allow yourself more free time."

"We are back to that already? I'll slack off when our cabin is done and not before."

Evelyn was on her knees in front of the fire, her hands to the crackling flames. "It sure gets chilly at night this high up."

"Wait until winter," Nate said. "We'll have ice hanging from our noses, it will be so cold."

"Speak for yourself, Pa. I won't step outside if that's the case." Evelyn bent over the pot and ladled a slab of venison onto a plate. Next to the venison she stacked two thick pieces of bread. "This is yours, I understand."

Nate accepted a fork and sat cross-legged with his back to his saddle. Truth to tell, he was famished. Winona handed him his tin cup brimming with steaming coffee and he savored a sip. "It won't be long before we can eat at a table in the comfort of our own home."

"I can't wait to have a room of my own again," Evelyn said. "The one place I can go and shut out the world."

"We all need a private place," Winona said.

His mouth bulging with venison, Nate glanced up. "A strange thing for you to say, seeing as how you were raised in a lodge." Tepees afforded no privacy whatsoever. Everything a person did was right out in front of everyone else.

"Whenever I wanted privacy, I would pull a blanket over my head," Winona said. "The others knew not to disturb me."

As Nate recollected, blankets also played an important part in Shoshone courtship. Maidens and their suitors stood outside at night under blankets and whispered sweet endearments, among other things. "You heard your daughter. She can't wait for our cabin to be done."

"She is young and the young do not have much patience," Winona said. "But an extra week or two will not hurt her."

Evelyn did not understand. "But we've already had to wait longer than everyone else. Aren't you as excited as I am about our new place?"

"Of course I am," Winona said. "But not at the expense of your father's health. Or haven't you noticed that he is exhausted?"

"Pa always works hard. It's his nature."

"Out of the mouths of babes." Nate smirked, but his wife was not in the mood to appreciate his humor.

"I'm no baby," Evelyn said. She looked from one to the other. "What the dickens is going on here, anyhow?"

"A mild disagreement," Nate explained.

"Your father will not do as I have asked," Winona said. "We have been married so long, he takes me for granted."

Nate tried another tack. "I need to get our cabin finished before the cold weather hits. This high up, it will be a lot earlier than we were used to along the foothills."

"Pa has a point," Evelyn said.

Winona did not say anything more until Nate had taken another sip and placed his cup on a flat rock beside him. "The grizzly will still be here whether you take two more weeks or four."

"It's not about the bear," Nate said. But it was; he knew it and she knew it and she knew he knew it.

Evelyn was enjoying their conversation. "Zach says he hasn't seen any sign of the griz for almost a month now. He thinks it crossed over into the valley to the west and might never come back."

"It will," Nate predicted. "Bears roam a large territory, is all."

Winona had her opening. "And you want our cabin finished so when the grizzly comes back, you will be free to carry out your insanity."

"Here we go again," Nate said.

"Just shoot the thing so we can get on with our lives," Winona urged. "Your son nearly lost his life to that bear. Didn't it teach you anything?"

"I've learned my wife doesn't have much confidence in me or she wouldn't brand my plan insane."

"Do not twist my words, husband. I speak with a straight tongue. Am I wrong to call fire hot? Or water wet? If not, then I am not wrong when I say I am not against your plan because I lack confidence in you."

"A fine distinction, if you ask me."

Evelyn shook her head. "I've never heard you two argue so much as you have over this stupid bear. Why can't you make up and be like you were before?"

"Because your father refuses to admit I am right and I will never admit I am wrong so long as I am right," Winona said.

"That made a lot of sense," Nate remarked, not without sarcasm. It was the wrong thing to do.

"So this is what we have come to? In all our years you have never treated me with so little disrespect." Winona stood, her eyes blazing with flames that were not reflections of the fire. "If this is how you want it, then I will say no more on the subject, ever." She clenched her fists. "Except that to call men pigheaded is an insult to pigs."

"Is that men in general or do you have a particular male in mind?" Nate asked.

Winona's response was to spin on her heel and stalk off into the dark along the lake.

"Shouldn't you go after her, Pa?" Evelyn asked.

"If I don't want to spend the rest of my life sleeping on the floor, I suppose I should." Nate reluctantly put down his plate and stood. "All I want is to do what's best. Why can't your mother and your brother see that?"

"Like Ma said, each of you thinks you are right. But you can't both be."

Nate hastened after Winona. She had not taken a gun, and at night meat eaters were afoot. He figured to catch up quickly, but she was moving under a full boiler of steam and he had to run to overtake her. "Hold up, will you?"

"No." Winona's hips were twitching so violently, she looked fit to bust from her dress.

"I'm sorry if I hurt your feelings."

"I want to be alone."

GET
4 FREE BOOKS!

You can have the best Westerns delivered to your door for less than what you'd pay in a bookstore or online. Sign up for one of our book clubs today, and we'll send you 4 FREE* BOOKS, worth $23.96, just for trying it out...with no obligation to buy, ever!

Authors include classic writers such as
LOUIS L'AMOUR, MAX BRAND, ZANE GREY
and more; PLUS new authors such as
COTTON SMITH, TIM CHAMPLIN, JOHNNY D. BOGGS
and others.

As a book club member you also receive the following special benefits:
- **30% OFF** all orders through our website & telecenter!
- **Exclusive access** to special discounts!
- **Convenient** home delivery and 10 days to return any books you don't want to keep.

There is no minimum number of books to buy,
and you may cancel membership at any time.
See back to sign up!

*Please include $2.00 for shipping and handling.

YES!

Sign me up for the Leisure Western Book Club and send my FOUR FREE BOOKS! If I choose to stay in the club, I will pay only $14.00* each month, a savings of $9.96!

NAME: _____

ADDRESS: _____

_____

TELEPHONE: _____

E-MAIL: _____

☐ **I WANT TO PAY BY CREDIT CARD.**

☐ VISA ☐ MasterCard ☐ DISCOVER

ACCOUNT #: _____

EXPIRATION DATE: _____

SIGNATURE: _____

Send this card along with $2.00 shipping & handling to:

Leisure Western Book Club
20 Academy Street
Norwalk, CT 06850-4032

Or fax (must include credit card information!) to: 610.995.9274.
You can also sign up online at www.dorchesterpub.com.

*Plus $2.00 for shipping. Offer open to residents of the U.S. and Canada only.
Canadian residents please call 1.800.481.9191 for pricing information.
If under 18, a parent or guardian must sign. Terms, prices and conditions subject to change. Subscription subject
to acceptance. Dorchester Publishing reserves the right to reject any order or cancel any subscription.

Nate snagged her sleeve but she shrugged loose. "You didn't bring your rifle or a pistol. It's not safe."

"Says the bear tamer."

"Damn it, Winona, enough is enough." Nate ran in front of her and planted himself in her path so she had no choice but to stop.

Winona went around him. "Now you swear at me too? Next you will beat me and insist I never set foot outside our cabin without your permission."

"That's going too far." Nate grabbed her wrist. "You will listen to me whether you want to or not." He had more to say, a lot more, but just then small waves began to lap the shore, one after the other. "What in the world?" The sky was cloudless, the wind not strong enough to account for them.

"It is our lake monster," Winona said.

"Our what?"

The waves grew until they were half a foot high and their slithery hiss as they broke on shore reminded Nate of the hiss of surf along the Oregon coast. But as quickly as they appeared, they subsided. Out on the lake a pale bubbly froth appeared, as if something large had submerged.

Nate wondered whether his eyes had played tricks on him. There had to be a logical explanation. In all the weeks they had been there, not once had he seen anything remotely similar.

"Maybe you would like to tame this beast, too." Pulling loose, Winona resumed walking.

"Will you cut it out?" Two strides, and Nate was beside her. "Please stop. I promise to drop the subject. I just want you back at the fire where it's safe."

"There is that word again," Winona said, but she

stopped and stood with her arms folded. "We *are* being childish, aren't we?"

Pulling her close, Nate gently embraced her. He kissed her cheek and her brow, placed his chin on top of her head, and quietly savored the feel and the warmth of her. It had been so long since they last enjoyed a tender moment, he had nearly forgotten how wonderful they were. After a long while he said softly, "I love you with all my heart, you know."

"And I love you."

Nate was afraid to say more. It might spoil the magic. He kissed her hair and her ear instead.

Winona cleared her throat. "I am reminded of the wagon train bound for the Oregon Country last year."

Confused, Nate tried to make sense of what that had to do with anything. As best he could recollect, they had come across the train while on a visit to the Shoshones, and stopped for a night at the wagon boss's request. A farmer from Ohio, the wagon boss had never been to Oregon and was eager to learn about the lay of the land. It had given Nate an idea he had yet to act on. "What about it?" he guardedly asked.

"There was a woman, a heavyset woman with her hair in a bun, in a calico dress. She had a husband and five children."

Nate vaguely remembered her. "Wasn't she the loud one? The one who wouldn't stop complaining about the heat and the dust and the food and everything else under the sun?"

"That is the one, yes."

"And?" Nate prompted when she did not go on.

"I am turning into her."

A laugh rose in Nate's throat but he smothered it

and said, "I must have missed something. You are not anything like that woman."

"I complain a lot these days," Winona said. "More than I ever used to. More than I should. When Evelyn does not do things as I want them done, I complain. When things do not go as well as I would like, I complain." She gazed into his eyes. "When you want to do something I am against, I complain."

"That's your right as a wife," Nate grinned, making light of it. "When a man does something stupid, his woman should point it out."

"There is more to it," Winona said. "I have changed. I am not the same woman you married."

Nate gave her a squeeze. "We all change. It's human nature. If we stayed the same our whole lives long, we might as well be lumps of clay."

"I want you to know that in the future I will not complain as much."

Nate had never thought of her as a chronic carper. Some women were. Some wives made their husbands miserable by constantly pointing out their faults and failings. For the man, every waking moment became a litany of his shortcomings; things he had not done, things he had not done right, things he should have done the way she wanted them done, on and on and on, without cease, as unrelenting as hail in a hailstorm.

Old Tom was the best example Nate could think of. A free trapper who took a Crow woman as his wife, Old Tom was browbeat without mercy. His woman wielded words as if they were a club, and beat him at every opportunity. Nearly every comment that came out of her mouth was critical. Old Tom could not do anything right, in her estimation. Amazingly, he put up with it. Old Tom took the verbal abuse as a matter of course and never became angry with her or criticized her in return. It was always, "Yes, dear," or "Whatever you say, dear."

At the time Nate had been too young to understand why a man would let himself be whipped raw day in and day out. Shakespeare had chuckled and said, "You have a heap to learn, Horatio. When it comes to some females, their tongues are daggers."

"But why does Old Tom take it?" Nate had asked in exasperation.

"Because he loves her. And in case you haven't heard, love is blind. If it wasn't, a lot more marriages would end before they really begin."

"Well, I wouldn't put up with it."

"It's easy to talk big when you're not being shot at," Shakespeare had replied. "But love makes a person do mighty strange things, things they would never do if they were in their right mind."

"So you're saying love is a form of lunacy?"

Shakespeare had lit up like a candle. "Why, that's a brilliant observation, if I do say so myself, and I'm glad I thought of it. Yes, love is a union of lunatics. Two people joined at the hip by a contagion."

"Oh? Now love is a disease?"

"In a sense. Think about it. Love makes you feel lightheaded. Love makes you hot and sweaty or cold and clammy. Love has all the symptoms of a disease so we might as well call it one."

"Love is more than that," Nate had maintained.

"Suit yourself. But it explains Old Tom. He's caught a disease for which there is no cure, so all he can do is suffer in silence. I was the same way once."

"Your first wife was like his?"

"She wasn't as bad. She would say nice things now and again to ease her conscience. But mainly I was always in the wrong and couldn't please her if I tried. I sure tried, too, disease-ridden as I was."

"Disease makes people sick. Disease kills people. Love doesn't do that. Love makes us feel good inside. Love is healthy for us."

"Spoken like the puppy you are," Shakespeare had grinned. "But when a man is chained to a woman with a dagger in her mouth, he gets stabbed from dawn until dusk. It eats away at him. And while it might not kill his body, it kills something worse. It kills his spirit. He becomes a shell of what he was. It would be sad if it weren't so damned self-indulgent."

"Now you've lost me," Nate admitted.

"Surely you've noticed that people have a natural knack for excusing everything they do? Things are never their fault. This or that makes them do what they do. In Old Tom's case, he called it love. I did, too, once. But now I see it for what it really is. Stupidity."

"That's harsh."

"Reality usually is. Always remember, Horatio. There are two ways of looking at the world, as it is, and as we think it is. The first path leads to misery. The second brings us the highest happiness we can know."

There were times, and that had been one of them, when McNair's ramblings left Nate more perplexed than enlightened. While he agreed that people did a lot of silly things in the name of love, he would never go so far as to brand it a disease, and he suspected that Shakespeare didn't really think it was, either, but was talking to stir him up. Still, it had given Nate considerable food for thought, and when he later married Winona, he worried for a while that she might turn into a shrew. But she never did. Not that she didn't take him to task when she felt it was warranted. But she wasn't one of those women who flayed the hides from their mates and then were upset if their men did not enjoy the experience.

Winona was talking to him.

"—you want to do, then I will support you as best I am able. But I still think you might get yourself killed."

"If it comes down to the griz or me, I won't hesitate. I want it to live, but I have no hankering to die."

Winona kissed him. "I have no hankering for you to die, either. On winter nights you come in handy."

"Only in the winter?" Nate asked, and kissed her long and hard.

When they broke for breath, Winona leaned her forehead on his broad chest and rested her hands on his shoulders.

"Please, husband. Take utmost care. You mean the world to your family and friends."

Nate thought of Evelyn and Zach and Lou and the McNairs, and wavered. It would be so simple to kill the grizzly and be done with it. But he heard himself say, "No need to fret. Things will turn out all right. You'll see."

But he wasn't fooling anyone. Not even himself.

Interregnum

The bear acknowledged no lord. The bear bowed to no master. It was complete in and of itself, answerable only to its own will, its own drives, its own urges. With one exception.

The bear's life was linked to the cycles of the seasons. The weather told it what to do and when to do it. Spring was for feasting on the replenished bounty. Summer was for lolling in the hot sun and lazing away warm nights. Autumn was for gorging so it would survive the long, cold months to follow.

This autumn was no different. The bear felt the brisk nip of the morning chill. It saw squirrels gathering acorns. It noticed V-shaped flights of honking geese wing south. It heard the bugling of bull elk and witnessed their mighty clashes. It sensed the change in the earth and the creatures that shared its domain, and felt a change within itself.

The bear returned to its home valley after being absent for a while. On its way over the high pass it spied gray tendrils near the lake and descended to investigate.

The bear seldom felt surprise, but it felt something akin to surprise now. Where before the lake shore had been smooth and flat and undisturbed, now three alien forms stood as if sprung from the soil like flowers. Only these were not plants. These were wood forms unlike any the bear ever beheld. The smoke came from what appeared to be stones stacked on top.

On a brisk autumn dawn the bear watched from concealment as part of the wood in one of the forms moved. An opening appeared. Out of it came a two-leg, the one with the black hair on its face. Black Hair walked around to the side, where a number of four-legs were penned in a rectangle of tree limbs. Black Hair began feeding the four-legs grass.

To the bear it was a mystery and a wonderment. The two-legs were always doing things no other creatures did. They were completely different from anything the bear ever knew. They did not act as prey, even if some two-legs did have the stink of fear about them when the bear charged.

The young one the bear had treed had not betrayed any fear whatsoever. To the contrary, the bear had sensed fury. That in itself was remarkable. Few creatures dared stand up to it. Far fewer dared to fight back as the young two-leg had done.

The bear had not forgotten the stick that made a loud noise and spat smoke. It also remembered the hide the young one had dropped from the tree, and how the hide clung so that it could not open its mouth. Suddenly Black Hair turned from the four-legs and gazed at the forest. At the exact strip of woods in which the bear stood. The bear was well hidden in the shadows. It was certain the two-leg did not know it was there. As was its custom, it had approached downwind so its scent would not give it away. Yet the Black Hair kept staring.

The bear growled. There was something about this particular two-leg that filled it with a vague unease.

Out of the opening came another of the strange creatures. This one was small and female and moved with a grace that reminded the bear of a young tawny cat. It showed its teeth to Black Hair and flitted about like a butterfly, chattering the whole while as a chipmunk would do.

The bear wondered how the small two-leg would taste. Young creatures were softer and more succulent than their parents. Fawns were so juicy and sweet, the bear preferred them to all else, even fish, of which it was exceptionally fond.

Now the young two-leg was strolling toward the forest. The bear tensed. If the little female came close enough, it would charge from cover and be on her before she could escape. Its nostrils flaring, it marked the narrowing distance between them.

Then Black Hair made a loud noise and gestured, and the young she turned and went back. For an instant the bear almost rushed out after her, but instinct held the bear in its place. Instinct, and the sight of the long stick Black Hair held.

The bear had seen enough. It melted into the vegetation. Thirsty, it headed for the beaver pond. There was always the possibility a beaver would stray too near land, but on this day the male beaver was across the water, gnawing at a tree, and spotted the bear before the bear spotted it. Almost immediately the male beaver entered the pond and proceeded to slap its tail on the surface to warn the other beavers they had an unwanted visitor.

The bear contented itself with slaking its thirst. The beaver swam toward the bear but prudently did not come too near. Veering toward its lodge, the male beaver dived with barely a ripple.

Once, when young, the bear had jumped in the pond and tried to get at the beaver family by ripping through their lodge. But the lodge was so sturdily constructed that by the time the bear tore through the wall, the beaver had escaped. The wasted effort taught the bear not to try again.

That was how life had always been for the bear. It learned through trial and error. Its mother had not been able to teach it all it needed to know before she died, so the bear had to find out for itself.

One of the things its mother never taught it about were the two-legs. The bear had never been so surprised as the first time it saw one. The two-leg had been old, and wore deer hide over its own skin, and had eagle feathers in its hair. The bear had watched as the two-leg climbed on a boulder and draped a colored hide over its shoulders, then spent the next couple of suns bleating like a mountain sheep and swaying with its upper limbs in the air. Overcome by curiosity, the bear had been content to go on watching until the old one roused and climbed weakly down from the boulder.

The two-leg was almost to the ground when the bear attacked. The two-leg cried out and thrust its upper limbs at the bear as if to ward the bear off, but the bear was many times bigger and many times heavier. The old one crumbled under a single blow, shattered bones jutting from its skin.

The odor of spilled blood had fueled the bear's hunger. But when it bit into the two-leg, it discovered the meat was stringy and bland. Plus, the bear kept getting pieces of deer hide in its mouth. After only a few bites it stopped eating. Annoyed, it swung a paw, and the old one's head separated from the old one's neck and rolled into the grass.

A couple of winters had passed, and the bear came on a party of two-legs in high timber. They were riding four-legs, a kind of creature the bear never beheld, and the bear shadowed them for several suns, learning all it could.

The two-legs were all male. All had red or yellow or blue streaks on their faces. All carried odd curved sticks that they used to send small straight sticks a great distance. The bear saw a buck brought down.

The two-legs had removed the hide and cut up the meat. Then they did the strangest thing of all. They somehow created a crackling orange heat that writhed as if alive, and hung the strips of meat over the heat.

After a while a new aroma reached the bear, an aroma that proved more than the bear could withstand. Roaring, it had rushed out of the night and been among them before they could grab their curved sticks. The young two-legs proved to be as helpless as the old two-leg had been. They were no match for the bear's teeth and claws. Within moments they were all dead or dying.

Their meat proved to be less stringy than the old

one's. Their bellies, in particular, were baskets of ripe organs. The bear feasted until gorged, and went off and slept. Later the bear came back for more, only to find that coyotes had paid the remains a visit in its absence and helped themselves to what meat was left.

So the bear went after the four-legged creatures the two-legs had ridden. The four-legs had fled in fright the night before. Catching up to them took considerable effort but the bear was eager to taste their flesh. It stalked them from sunrise until sunset and still did not overtake them. Hunger impelled it on. Under a canopy of stars the bear came to a stream and there, bedded down for the night, were the long-manes.

The bear softly padded close enough to hear their steady breathing. A roar petrified them for the instant it took the bear to crash in among them. The scent of a female drew the bear like honey, and it tore into a mare like a whirlwind with claws. Within seconds the carnage was complete; the mare's neck was ripped wide open and both her front legs broken.

She was delicious, but not as appealing as the two-legs that rode her.

From then on the bear was on the lookout for more two-legs but they were rare and hard to find. Twice it came across their spoor but on both occasions they had too substantial a lead.

Not that long ago the bear killed one, though, and found several bodies to devour. It was when the bear first saw Black Hair. Now Black Hair had returned, and the bear's valley had been invaded by other two-legs.

The bear was determined to feast on them or drive them out before another moon went by.

Midway up a slope strewn with wildflowers, the

bear twisted its huge head to look back. Far down the mountain, something moved. One instant it was there, then in a blink of the bear's eyes, nothing.

The bear waited to see if it reappeared. After a suitable interval, convinced it had been the play of the shadows and sunlight, the bear lumbered on. Presently it came to a rise and once again looked back, and this time there could be no mistake. It was not shadow and sunlight.

One of the two-legs was following it.

To the bear this was confusing. Always in the past, it did the stalking. To be stalked was new, and not to its liking.

The bear watched awhile. This time the two-leg made no attempt to hide. Soon the bear saw that it was Black Hair, astride a big black long-mane.

Rearing onto its hind legs for a better view, the bear was bewildered when Black Hair raised a limb and showed his teeth and yipped much like a coyote or wolf would yip. This, too, was novel, and added to the bear's puzzlement.

The bear dropped onto all fours, turned, and broke into a run. For short distances it was as fleet of paw as any creature in the wild, and it ran now at its top speed, crashing through the underbrush with no regard to the noise it made. It had gone as far as a cub could run without tiring when it halted, raised its head to sniff, then made off into pines on its right. Moving as silently as a bobcat, it circled in a wide loop that would bring it up on Black Hair from behind, a ploy it used when it hunted deer and elk and other creatures.

The bear had done it so many times that the execution was second nature. When it had gone as far as it deemed necessary, it angled toward its own trail, its nose flaring as it sought the two-leg's scent. And there the scent was! Circling back had worked. Now all that was left was the rush and the kill.

But when the bear came to where it could see its back trail, the two-leg was not there. The bear looked up the mountain and then down the mountain but Black Hair and the big long-mane had vanished.

It could not be and yet it was. Wary of a trap, the bear moved forward until it came to its own tracks. Beside them were the tracks of the black long-mane. He followed them, stopping often to sniff and listen.

The bear expected to come on Black Hair any moment. But on it climbed, with no sign of the lone-mane or its rider. Then the long-mane's tracks angled away from the bear's, and the bear lifted its huge head in wonderment. The hunt was not going as it should. This had never happened before. Countless creatures the bear had hunted, and never had its quarry behaved like this.

Off amid the trees was the long-mane. Black Hair raised a limb and showed his teeth and yipped as he had earlier, and while the gesture and the yip held no meaning to the bear, the bear sensed that to the two-leg, the hunt was a source of great pleasure. This, too, was unforeseen and beyond the scope of the bear's experience, and because of that, all the more unsettling.

For a reason it could not fathom, the bear thought of the great cat that lived in the next valley, a male that had seen ten winters or more, and next to the bear, was the most fearsome creature in the wild. One morning, many sunrises past, the bear had come on the great cat in a meadow. That alone was unusual, as the great cat so seldom showed itself in the open. It was prancing and leaping about as a kitten might do, and the bear was set to hurtle from ambush when it saw another creature in the tall grass.

A marmot had been caught too far from its burrow. Blood, and a bad limp, told the bear that the marmot was hurt and one of its legs was useless. The marmot could not move fast, it could barely walk, yet still it kept trying to escape.

The great cat would not let it. The cat would swat it and nip it, then let the marmot totter a little ways, then pounce and swat and nip and let it totter in another direction, playing with it as a bear cub might play with a bone.

Black Hair was doing to the bear as the great cat had done to the marmot.

The insight came as a sudden knowing, as so much of the bear's insights did. With the knowing came resentment. The bear did not like being played with. It was the lord of its domain. It was always the hunter, never the hunted.

Roaring, the bear gave chase. It was too far from the long-mane to catch it, but not so far that the bear could not drive it off and teach the arrogant two-leg that the bear was master of the valley.

But once again things were not as they should be. Black Hair did not flee in stark fright. Neither did the long-mane's scent carry with it the raw tang of rank fear. Neither the two-leg nor the four-leg were scared.

As if it had slammed into a boulder, the bear came to a stop. It did not like this. Instinct urged it to put distance between the two-leg and itself, but it hesitated. If only it could get close enough to use it claws, then would it teach the two-leg its rightful place in the order of all creatures.

Suddenly Black Hair raised the long stick he held. He pointed the long stick at the bear, and the bear heard a sound that made the bear think of the crack of twig but was not quite the same.

The next sound was much louder, a blast like thunder accompanied by a cloud of smoke, and a buzzing as of a large bee. Something struck a pine next to the bear and slivers exploded like porcupine quills, stinging the bear's nose and cheeks and eyes. A hole appeared where there had not been a hole moments ago.

Wheeling, the bear sped up the mountain. It sensed that whatever hit the tree could do to him as it had done to the pine. In some mysterious way the two-leg could inflict harm from a distance with the long stick, just as the other two-legs could inflict harm with their curved sticks. Where the sticks came from, and how they could do what they did, was as much of a mystery as everything else about the two-legs.

When the bear grew tired it slowed to a walk. It had left the long-mane far behind and was free to go on prowling the valley in search of sustenance.

Then a whinny was lifted aloft on the wind, and the bear looked down to find Black Hair and the long-mane climbing after it.

Fury fought with uncertainty, and uncertainty won. The bear ran to the crest and down the opposite slope. It was not bound for any particular place. It was running to lose the strange stalker.

The bear crossed a ribbon of water and started up the next mountain. It traveled almost to the top before it stopped and shifted its ponderous bulk. The two-leg was still back there.

Enough of running. The bear faced its pursuer and vented a growl that would cause most lesser creatures to cower in abject terror. But not Black Hair or the long-mane. Undaunted, they came on, but stopped far enough below that the bear could not reach them in a rush.

Once more the two-leg motioned and made the same odd yip. Once more the long stick was raised to the two-leg's shoulders. The *boom* and the billow of a cloud of smoke were simultaneous.

The ground in front of the bear erupted. Dirt showered its jaw and mouth. The bear saw a hole, much like the hole in the pine, and in another flash of insight realized that the long stick was somehow much like a buffalo's horn or an elk's antler. It put holes in things. In trees, in the ground. And in bears.

It loped up the mountain and into the thickest trees it could find. Once in deep shadow, it stopped and turned at bay. It had run as far as it was going to. Let the two-leg come.

Time passed, and although the bear intently watched its back trail and the surrounding woodland, Black Hair and the lone-mane did not appear. The bear stayed where it was. The two-leg had not given up. Not after chasing him so far.

More time dragged by. The bear was tired and would like to nap but sleep could wait. So could tending to its thirst and hunger.

So much had happened that only now did the bear seek to make sense of it. The two-leg's purpose was a mystery. If Black Hair was after the bear's life, why had Black Hair put holes in the pine and in the ground?

Confusion reined. And more resentment. The bear did not like being treated as the big cat had treated the marmot. It was accustomed to being in control.

More time crept by like a snail. The bear did not understand where the two-leg had gotten to. It sniffed a lot, relying on its ally, the wind, to tell it where Black Hair was, but for once its ally was of no value.

The bear always stalked from downwind when it was after prey, so perhaps the two-leg was doing the same. Gliding to where the Black Hair should be, the bear was disappointed to find only foliage.

More confused than ever, the bear left the dense cover. The top of the mountain beckoned. Once there it would make for a pass into the next valley and stay until it was sure the two-leg had lost interest.

The bear climbed steadily. Birds flitted from its path and squirrels fled through the treetops, chittering in fear. Once a doe bounded off, bleating.

The bear hardly noticed.

At the pass it paused to scour the terrain below. There was still no sign of the two-leg. Grunting in satisfaction, the bear entered the narrow pass. On either side reared ramparts of stone twice its height. Here it was dark and cool, and the bear was tempted to stop and rest. But it passed on through and out the other side and down a sparsely covered slope to timber.

The bear was in one of four valleys connected to the bear's own. Of them all, it was the smallest, and game was not as plentiful. Still, there was more than enough to sustain the bear a good while.

It had gone a short way into the forest when fortune smiled on it. From below came the distinct scent of elk. The bear had not enjoyed elk meat in a long time, and its mouth watered at the prospect.

Elk were big creatures. They stood as tall as the bear. The larger males weighed nearly as much, and their meat was tasty.

But the bear had to remember that their many-tined antlers made for formidable weapons. The bear once witnessed a clash between a bull elk and a pack of wolves. The wolves tried again and again to dart in close and bring the elk down by tearing at its legs. But each time the wolves charged, the elk met them with its antlers. Eventually the pack gave up and went after easier prey.

The bear was a ghost amid the firs. At that time of day elk were usually bedded down. Come evening, and they would venture out to graze.

On the bear's left was a tree partially stripped of bark. Elk routinely marked their territories in that manner, the cows by stripping the bark with their teeth, the bulls by rubbing the bark with their antlers or their muzzles. The bear had also known elk to mangle saplings by twisting until the saplings splintered.

Despite their size, elk rarely made noise when they were on the go. Unlike their deer cousins, they moved as silently as the bear, and as fast, which made stalking them a challenge.

The bear knew the habits of all the creatures with which it shared the wilderness. It had to. Its survival depended on consuming enough to sustain its massive body. It was always in need of food. Meat was its favorite—juicy, red, dripping meat—but it would eat virtually anything that interested it: bugs, berries,

roots, even the fungus few creatures would touch. The
bear also ate carrion. Whenever it came on the kills of
other creatures, be it a cat or wolves or a wolverine, it
helped itself. The cats and wolves might take exception but they never contested the loss.

Wolverines always did. They always stood up to the
bear and resisted with a ferocity that rivaled its own.
The last time the bear began to help itself to a deer
killed by the pair of wolverines in its home valley, they
drove the bear off.

A sharp snort brought the bear to a halt. The elk
were near. The bear probed the vegetation and soon
distinguished the telltale silhouette of a cow. The rest
had to be nearby.

Another snort, from a thicket, was the first inkling
the bear had that the breeze had shifted. Some of the
elk had caught its scent. The next few moments would
be crucial.

Suddenly the vegetation crackled, and out of the
greenery rose a bull. It looked right at the bear. The
loudest snort yet burst from the elk's throat, serving as
a signal to the rest. On all sides they rose, male and female, old and young. None of the elk moved. They
were waiting to see what the bear would do.

The bear did not keep them waiting to find out. It
flew toward the nearest, a young bull that bolted. The
rest raced off every which way.

The bear stayed focused on the young bull. A burst
of speed brought it to the bull's side and a swing of its
forepaw left red furrows on the elk's flank. But the bull
did not break stride.

The woods became a blur. The bear snapped at the
elk's rear leg but missed. Its eyes wide, the bull cut to

the left and then the right. The bear stayed glued to its hoofs.

The elk must have realized it could not shake the bear. A few more flying bounds brought the bull to a clearing where it whirled with its head lowered. Only a swift sidestep by the bear kept it from being impaled on the bull's antlers. The bear lunged at the elk's hindquarters but the bull swung to meet it and the bear had to retreat. The bear circled, the elk turning with every step so its antlers were always between them.

The bear swung to the right and the bull turned with it. In mid-stride the bear changed direction, going to the left instead, and before the bull could adjust, the bear slammed broadside into it. Swept off its legs, the elk crashed to the ground. Frantic, it tried to scramble back up.

The bear sheared its teeth into the bull's exposed throat. Warm, sweet blood spurted in a geyser. The bear clamped its iron jaws fast. A wildy thrashing hoof struck it but did no harm. The tips of the bull's antlers brushed its shoulder, narrowly missing the bear's eyes. Then the thrashing ceased and the bull lay still, its tongue lolling from lifeless lips.

The bear stepped back. Now it could feed. A sound drew its gaze to the woods. Another elk, the bear assumed.

But it was Black Hair.

Chapter Seven

It was insane. It was immature. It was preposterous. But Nate King was having fun. He was playing a cat-and-mouse game that could turn deadly at any moment, yet enjoying himself immensely.

The thrill has a lot to do with it. The heart-pumping heady excitement of baiting a grizzly, the most fearsome beast in all creation. Of doing what no man had ever done. Doing what no one had ever *attempted*.

Now, sitting astride his bay with his Hawken in the crook of an elbow, Nate nearly laughed at the grizzly's expression. It was downright comical. The bear was stunned to see him. Waving, he smiled and yelled, "I'm back! Did you miss me?"

The silver-tip took several shambling steps toward him, then stopped, apparently unsure of what to do.

"Nice elk you have there!" Nate hollered. "Mind sharing the meat or are you a glutton?"

The grizzly tossed its huge head from side to side, as grizzlies sometimes did when harassed by flies or bees. It turned back to the bull, buried its teeth in the elk's neck, and commenced feasting, paying no more attention to Nate.

"We can't have that, can we?" Nate asked the bay, then gigged it a few yards to his left. Once he had a clear view of the bear's head, he drew rein, tucked the Hawken's stock to his shoulder, and took a slow, deliberate bead. "That griz is going to hate me for this," he predicted, and fired.

The heavy lead ball cored the elk's forehead, showering bone and hair and blood on the grizzly. In reflex, the bear sprang back, then glowered at Nate and snarled.

"I sure am a caution," Nate said. Grinning, he waved, then hauled on the reins as the grizzly, beside itself with rage, shot toward the bay like a gigantic cannonball shot out of a cannon.

Nate had prudently stayed far enough from the clearing that the bear could not possibly catch him unless the bay fell, and he was careful to avoid all logs, boulders and entanglements.

Laughing for glee, Nate galloped down the mountain. He was being childish, but he did not care. It was plain and pure fun, the likes of which he had not experienced since he was knee-high to a colt.

A roar signaled that the grizzly had halted. It recognized the futility of giving chase. But, Lordy, it was mad. It bit at a tree. It roared several more times. It tore at the earth with its claws.

A safe distance lower, Nate sat and laughed. "Serves

you right for trying to eat my son!" he shouted. "You've got to learn to leave us be."

The bear stopped roaring and looked at him with its brow puckered as if it were deep in thought.

Could it think? Nate wondered. He sometimes speculated on exactly how intelligent animals were. It was only natural, given that he dealt with all sorts of creatures, day in and day out.

Birds, for instance, appeared to be fairly bright, for the most part. Ravens and crows were exceptionally intelligent; he once saw a crow use a stick to get at some insects. The dumbest bird, in Nate's estimation, were turkeys. They had bodies as big as stoves and brains the size of peas. He once saw seven of them try to get out of the rain by ringing a pine no bigger than a wood box and sticking their heads under its thin branches, which offered no protection at all.

Lizards showed a glimmer of savvy, but snakes, as far as Nate could discern, acted and reacted on pure reptilian instinct, and nothing else.

Mammals were a mixed bunch. Foxes, wolves and coyotes were unbelievably crafty. Prairie dogs and gophers did not have intellects worth bragging about, but the cat family sure did. Bobcats, lynxes and mountain lions were deviously clever, but their cleverness was all of a kind: devoted solely to stealth.

Bears were a puzzlement. At times they showed no more brilliance than a tree stump. At other times they did things that demonstrated they were savvier than most animals when they put their minds to it.

Nate was convinced grizzlies were smarter than black bears. His many encounters of the ursine variety had taught him never to underestimate their intelligence. Or their sheer brute brawn. They were, without a doubt, the most powerful animal he'd ever come across.

The grizzly above him was turning back toward the clearing but moving much more slowly than it ordinarily would and casting repeated glances down the slope.

Nate suspected the bear was hoping he would follow too closely and give it the opportunity to rend him limb from limb but he stayed where he was. Smiling, he waved and called up, "It won't be that easy, gargantuan." He liked that word. "Gargantuan. I think that is what I will call you from now on since you are just about the biggest griz I have ever seen."

Just about. Once, decades ago, Nate tangled with another giant griz. Known as the Father Of All Bears to the Indians, they claimed it was a relict of antediluvian times when, according to the Shoshones and others, all the animals were much larger than they were now.

Not that the size mattered. All grizzlies were innately ferocious and capable of the most savage violence when provoked, and too often when not provoked. A kernel of knowledge Nate reminded himself he would do well to keep constantly in mind.

Gargantuan came to the clearing, and the dead bull elk. It resumed feeding. With its great teeth it tore off strips of hide so it could get at the soft meat underneath.

Nate approached to within the same distance as before. While the bear ate, he reloaded his Hawken. He did not shoot. But he did point the rifle at the grizzly, and the beast immediately stopped eating and stepped back as if expecting him to shoot. "You're catching on," Nate hollered.

Gargantuan bent to its meal.

Squinting at the sun, Nate calculated that if he wanted to make it to the cabin by dark, he must start back soon. "It's been an interesting day," he bellowed to the bear, and was ignored.

Interesting in more ways than one. The existence of the pass had been a welcome discovery. Nate had figured there would be a few up among the peaks, and he needed to know exactly where they were if he was to safeguard his family and friends. He had not come across sign of Indians but that did not mean they weren't out there somewhere, either in this valley or the next, and might present a threat.

The bear was engrossed in gorging.

"See you tomorrow maybe," Nate shouted, and reined around. The griz lifted its huge head and watched until the vegetation swallowed him.

Nate brought the bay to a gallop and held it at that pace until they were across the valley floor and climbing toward the pass. He would not put it past the griz to come after him but he reached the summit without incident.

Rock ramparts, broken only by the gap, separated the two valleys as effectively as would a giant wall. It occurred to Nate that all it would take to seal the valleys off, one from the other, was an appropriately placed keg of powder.

That thought sparked another. An idea so brilliant that Nate nearly reined up in surprise. A way to impress on the griz that it must leave them alone or suffer dire consequences.

Sunset transformed the western sky into a fiery patchwork of red, yellow and orange. The lake shimmered like a giant jewel. Ducks winged in from the east to land on the still water, while to the north the golden eagle and its mate soared. High to the northwest the glacier shone like a greenish white prism.

"Have you ever seen anything so beautiful?" Nate asked the bay. He had half a mile to go when another rider materialized out of the trees leading a pack horse with a buck tied over its back.

"You're still alive. Will wonders never cease."

"I expect sarcasm from Shakespeare, son. Not from you."

Zach chuckled and tugged on the lead rope. "The question to ask is whether that damn griz is still breathing?"

"Afraid so," Nate answered. "Although it won't be as anxious to make a meal of us after I get through."

"Or so you hope." Zach sighed and sadly shook his head. "I never thought I would live to see the day when you did something as loco as this."

"And I never thought I would live to see the day when my family would criticize me to death."

"Pardon us for caring, Pa," Zach said. "But I'll drop it if you want me to."

"I would be grateful."

They rode in silence until they were clear of the forest and the lake spread before them in all its dazzling emerald glory.

"I saw fresh wolverine sign today," Zach mentioned. "Two of them, up near the glacier."

"You went that high after deer?"

"I was exploring. There's a lot we don't know about

this valley. Our old one we knew inside out. We should get to know this one just as well."

Nate agreed. "You say there were two?"

"A male and a female. Big ones. A lot bigger than that one Ma killed when I was little." Zach gazed to the northwest. "I got close to the glacier. It's bigger than it looks from down here. Must be half as long as the lake. And there is something inside it."

"How do you mean, inside?"

"Something in the ice. I could see it. A dark shape. Some critter, I reckon, frozen solid long ago when the glacier was formed."

"Just so it stays there," Nate joked. "We'll have to go up together some time. I'd like a gander at it." He arched an eyebrow at his oldest. "We haven't jawed much these past weeks, being so busy and all. How does Lou like her new cabin? And what about you? Are you happy here?"

"Louisa likes the cabin just fine. The rooms are bigger than those in our last place, and she doesn't have to tote water as far. Plus, she likes being close to Ma and Sis and Blue Water Woman. Yesterday they got together and spent all morning flapping their gums."

"Females who like to gab. Imagine that."

"As for me, I'd be happy most anywhere there is enough game for the supper pot and enough wilderness for a man to roam as the urge moves him." Zach breathed deeply of the brisk twilight air. "You picked a good place. We shouldn't be bothered by hostiles or whites."

"Too soon to tell," Nate said. He told about the pass the grizzly had led him through. "We need to find out if there are others. Gargantuan knows, I bet, since it has been here so long."

119

Zach twisted in his saddle. "Gargantuan? Please don't tell me you have given the grizzly a name."

"Why not? We name dogs and cats, don't we?"

Zach's shoulders shook but he had the courtesy not to laugh out loud. "If you think I am going to treat that bear as if it's a kitten, you have another think coming. Or have you forgotten it tried to turn me into griz droppings?"

"I haven't forgotten a thing," Nate assured him. "But it hasn't attacked any of us since, and if I have a say, it never will again."

"Around and around we go," Zach said. "There is one other thing, though. When I was up near the glacier, I saw smoke over the divide."

"You're sure?" Nate asked, suddenly alarmed. Sometimes clouds resembled smoke, particularly on rainy days when the clouds hovered close to the ground.

"It was a long ways off but I'm as sure as can be. It had to be Indians. But who? They can't be Shoshones or Crows. Utes, neither." Zach paused. "Why are you smiling, Pa?"

"I had almost forgotten what the wilderness is like. Our old valley was so tame, it would do for a nunnery."

"You sound like Shakespeare."

As circumstance would have it, Nate's mentor was riding toward Nate's cabin, spied them, and veered to accompany them the rest of the way.

"How now, you scoundrels!" McNair bellowed with a grand wave. "What tidings bring you from France?"

"Where in blazes does he think we are, Pa?"

"Pretend he makes sense and your life will be easier," Nate advised. To Shakespeare he called, "The king sends his greetings and the queen wants to know what you did with her corset."

McNair indulged in lusty mirth. "Well, now you speak like a good child and a true gentleman," he quoted. "How green you are and fresh in this old world."

"If I live to be a hundred—" Zach muttered.

"Hush, son."

Shakespeare reined in beside Nate's bay. "How now, Horatio? Thy humble servant vows obedience and humble service to the point of death." He gave a mock bow. "How fares your bear?"

"The question of the day," Nate said.

"That is answer enough. But I see you don't have a few scratches to mark the occasion."

"You are worse than my family."

Shakespeare idly stroked his beard. "You would fault them because of their love for thee? Love is too precious not to be acknowledged as the treasure it truly is."

"Trust is precious, too," Nate responded.

"Touché. A hit, a very palpable hit. I am justly killed with my own treachery." Shakespeare leaned over and patted Nate's arm. "But the important thing is we are fond enough of you to worry. So quit your bellyaching, you ungrateful whelp."

At that, Zach laughed.

"See what I mean?" Nate said. "Bellyaching comes naturally when everyone gangs up on you."

Shakespeare winked at Zach. "We'll hear no more. Pursue him to his house, and pluck him thence, lest his infection, being of catching nature, spread further."

"I surrender," Nate said.

"A beastly ambition, which the gods grant thee to attain to. If thou wert the lion, the fox would beguile thee. If thou wert the lamb, the fox would eat thee. If thou wert the fox, the lion would suspect thee, when peradventure thou wert accused by the ass."

Zach looked at his father. "What in God's name is he talking about?"

"Either I should never give up," Nate guessed, "or I'm a loon."

"Thou art a scholar," Shakespeare said. "Let us therefore eat and drink."

"Finally, something I understand," Zach said. "Unless by eat and drink that bard of yours meant something else."

"Nay, by my troth, I know not. But I know to be up late is to be up late."

"Shoot me and put me out of my misery, Pa."

Nate laughed as he had not laughed since the move, and realized that for the first time in too long a time he was really and truly happy with himself and with his life. "Will wonders never cease."

"What's that, Horatio?" Shakespeare asked. "Mumbling ill becomes a gentleman of your fine distinction. Whisper if you must, or if you have excess breath, shout, but preserve us from mumbling."

"Only your bard would write something as silly as that," Zach interjected.

"First, it was original with me, and second, Old William S. is not my bard, he was and is a bard for the ages, for then and now and all the nows to come."

"Please shoot me, Pa. I'll even lend you my pistol."

"How now, wool-sack, what mutter you?"

By then they arrived at Nate's cabin. Winona was out the door before Nate brought the bay to a stop. The instant he dismounted, she embraced him, pressing her warm lips to his neck.

"You are still alive!"

"No griz can kill me," Nate joked.

Winona was not amused. Stepping back, she said severely, "I was worried sick, husband. The next time you go out after the bear, I am going with you."

Nate began walking the bay toward the corral. "We have been all through this. I must do it alone."

"Why? If the purpose is to train the bear to avoid people, the more people involved, the better."

"She has a point," Shakespeare said. He had dismounted and was following them.

"It's safer with only me," Nate said. Since it was his idea, he did not feel justified in having the others share the risk.

"I want to hear all about your day," Winona said. "What you did, and especially what the bear did."

"Judging for yourself, is that it?"

"I am your wife. I have that right when your life is at stake."

Shakespeare said, "I came over to hear how it went, too. It should be almost as entertaining as going to a circus."

"And what is that supposed to mean?" Nate asked, but then held up a hand. "Wait. Don't tell me. I don't want to know. You will only poke more fun at me."

"Why, Horatio, you wound me to the quick. Name one time in all these years I have made light of you."

"Only one of the four thousand?"

Shakespeare put a hand to his chest in a mock exaggeration of being stricken. "To think that I would live so long as to hear such slander from your barbed tongue! And me, the soul of discretion and propriety."

"The only thing you are the soul of," Nate said while opening the corral gate, "is the stuff that comes out the hind end of this horse."

"God help thee, shallow man," McNair quoted. "God make incision in thee, thou art raw."

"The Almighty would take my side. He takes pity on the abused. You would be lucky if He doesn't strike you with lightning."

Shakespeare snorted like a riled billy goat. "There is no terror in your threats. For I am arm'd so strong in honesty that they pass by me as the idle wind, which I respect not."

"Is honesty brown these days?" Nate grinned.

"You are a knave, a rascal, an eater of broken meats; a base, proud, shallow, beggarly, three-suited, hundred-pound, filthy worsted-stocking knave. A lily-livered, glass-gazing, super-serviceable, finical rogue."

"I'm all that?"

"Hush, whelp. I am not done yet." Shakespeare took a breath. "You art nothing but the composition of a knave, beggar, coward, panderer, and the son and heir of a mongrel bitch. One whom I will beat into clamorous whining if thou deni'st the least syllable of thy addition."

"Touchy today, are we?" Nate set to stripping the saddle and saddle blanket. "I bet the only reason you are here is because Blue Water Woman kicked you out of your cabin."

"Shall quips and sentences and these paper bullets of the brain awe a man from the career of his humor?"

"Is there no end?" Nate said.

Winona was smiling at their exchange. "Among my people two warriors never insult one another as you two do. They would come to blows."

"Flinging barbs is an ages-old tradition with our race," McNair mentioned. "It comes from suckling too long at our mothers' teats."

Nate nearly dropped the saddle. "That is the most ridiculous thing you have ever said. And I will thank you not to bring up teats in the presence of my wife."

"Why? She hasn't ever seen any?" But Shakespeare took Winona's hand and bent one knee. "My apologies, fair madam, if I have inadvertently offended thee by my overbold discourse."

"Not at all, kind sir. I am well familiar with teats. I see a pair every time I look in the mirror."

"Winona!" Nate exclaimed, embarrassed.

"Oh, don't be silly, husband. Were it a stranger I would be offended. But Shakespeare is family."

"Even so, you would never catch me talking about his wife's teats," Nate grumbled. "Some subjects should always be off limits."

"A notion I have never quite understood," Shakespeare said, serious now. "Why are bodily functions and intimate relations between a man and a woman taboo when we all have bodily functions and intimate relations are one of our prime enjoyments in life?"

"Some things are too private to talk about," Nate offered. "And making babies is at the top of the list."

"Only the human race," Shakespeare sighed. "One of the most beautiful experiences we can have, and we hide it under a bushel."

"A good place to stop is right now."

McNair leaned against the corral rails. "You are a man in stature but an infant at heart. But never fear. I will desist, if only to spare us your righteous indignation."

"There are days," Nate said, "when I dearly desire to beat you with a rock."

Shakespeare chortled and winked at Winona. "Baiting him is no challenge. It's like dangling a plump worm in front of a hungry catfish."

"Speaking of hungry," Nate said.

"I have supper on," Winona responded. "Our visitors are welcome to stay if they want. There is stew enough for all."

"I already ate," Shakespeare said, "but I wouldn't mind sticking around to prick your thick-headed half with his own inanities."

Nate gazed at the ground. "There must be a rock around here somewhere."

At that juncture Zach came around the corner of the cabin. He was still on the zebra dun. A strange look on his face, he drew rein. "So tell me, Pa. Do you reckon it went well with that bear of yours today? Gargantuan, as you call him?"

"He has given the bear a name?" Winona asked in astonishment.

"I think it went extremely well, yes," Nate answered. "Why do you ask?"

Zach pointed toward the woods. "Because Gargantuan followed you home."

Chapter Eight

There are occasional moments in the lives of men when circumstances lead to complete and utter astonishment. Astonishment so profound, all the man can do is stand and gape in dumfounded silence. Such was the case when Nate King strode to the corral gate and beheld the mammoth beast he thought he had left far up in the high country.

"Husband?" Winona said when he continued to stare in stunned bewilderment.

"It must be love," Shakespeare McNair quipped. "That there is a she-bear, unless I've gone blind. You have a rival, Winona. She has traipsed to your doorstep to court your man."

Zach cackled merrily. "Uncle Shakespeare, you come up with the craziest of notions sometimes."

McNair was regarding Nate with amusement twinkling in his eyes. "So you have named her Gargantuan? I can't say as it's the most flattering name for a female I've ever heard. Maybe it should be Gargantu-ana, given her gender."

"You are no help," Winona said. "What does the bear want? Why is it just standing there looking at us?"

"Who can explain romance?" Shakespeare rejoined.

Nate shook himself, as a man rousing from a stupor, and stepped from the corral, his Hawken in both hands. "This can't be good."

"What was your first clue?" Shakespeare asked. "If our valley is a democracy, I vote we kill her. Right this instant. Before she wreaks havoc with ours and us."

Zach leaned forward on his saddle. "Since you've trained that griz to heel, Pa, are you fixing to teach it to fetch, too?"

Now it was Shakespeare's turn to laugh uproariously, then to declare, "Zachary, that was marvelous. Between the two of us, he'll want to pull out his hair."

Wheeling, Nate walked to the bay. He did not bother saddling. Gripping its mane, he swung up, flicked the reins, and rode bareback out the gate.

"Where do you think you are going?" Winona asked.

Nate did not answer. He made straight for the fringe of vegetation a hundred yards away, and the great hulking form that seemed to have rooted itself in place. The bear watched him approach with a disturbing calmness.

Hoofs drummed, and Zach and Shakespeare trotted up on either side of the bay. "What's the big idea, Horatio?" the white-haired frontiersman demanded. "We have as much stake in this as you do."

"I can try to bring it down from here," Zach proposed.

"No," Nate said. They were still eighty yards out.

They needed to be a lot closer for the ball to have a lethal effect. If all they did was wound it, they would have an enraged berserker to deal with.

"Damned peculiar, this Gargantuana of yours," Shakespeare remarked. "Her following you bodes ill."

"Maybe we can scare it off." Nate aimed at the ground in front of the grizzly but he did not squeeze the trigger until forty yards separated them. His aim was true. The earth in front of the bear exploded in a dirt geyser. The last time Nate did that, the grizzly had fled. This time, incredibly, the bear did not so much as blink.

"Arrogant cuss," Shakespeare said.

"I still say I can bring it down," Zach urged.

Nate was reloading. "When we are close enough," he proposed, "all three of us will shoot on my signal."

"How close is that?" Zach asked.

Before Nate could answer, the issue was rendered moot by the grizzly, which, belying its massive bulk, abruptly turned and melted into the undergrowth with an amazing rapidity.

"After it!" Zach cried, and applied his heels so hard to the zebra dun that the dun fairly leaped in pursuit.

"Son! Wait!" Nate cried, but his breath was wasted on ears fired with the zeal of youth. Nate applied his own heels, anxious to stop Zach before his son reached the trees. But the dun, though smaller than the bay, was fleeter of hoof. Within moments Zach raced pell-mell into the greenwood, compelling Nate to holler, "Wait for us, consarn you!"

Shakespeare's white mare was neck-and-neck with the bay. "We can't let him get out of sight!"

Nate did not intend to. It was his fault the grizzly

was there, and he would not have his son's blood on his hands. Spurring the bay to its utmost, he again yelled for Zach to stop but Zach again ignored him.

Of the grizzly there was no trace. It might be in full flight. It might be luring them deep into the woods for the purpose of turning on them and rending them to ribbons.

"Damn that boy," Nate fumed.

Zach was an excellent rider. He had sat his first pony about the same time he learned to walk, and as a boy had spent as many hours on horseback as on foot. The speed with which he negotiated the closely spaced trees was remarkable.

Nate was too anxious for his son's safety to admire Zach's skill. As usual, his offspring was too reckless for his own good.

"Hold up!" Nate tried again, and was pleasantly delighted when his oldest suddenly hauled on the zebra dun's reins.

"Where did that critter get to?" Zach looked around in confusion. "It can't just disappear."

Nate begged to differ. Grizzlies were ghosts when they wanted to be. He reined to a stop next to the zebra dun, and snapped, "Were you trying to get yourself killed? Don't ever pull a hare-brained stunt like that again."

With a crash of underbrush, Shakespeare drew rein. His old mare was breathing heavily but pranced as if eager to keep going. "Let me guess. We lost a bear the size of a steamboat?"

"There have to be tracks," Zach said, casting about. "We'll track the thing down, and that will be that."

"Not at night we won't," Nate observed. The sun had relinquished the sky to gathering twilight and soon it would be too dark to see much of anything. "We'll have to wait until morning."

"We can track it by torchlight," Zach proposed.

Shakespeare shook his head. "Only if you have a death wish. A griz during the day is bad enough. A griz at night would be unstoppable."

And so, much to Zach's disgust, they turned homeward.

Nate road in silence. He was wrestling with his new problem, namely, what to do about the bear now that it had thrown a fur-lined gauntlet in his face? He was convinced the grizzly meant them harm. His attempts to persuade it to leave them alone had done the exact opposite.

Nate hoped he was wrong. He hoped the sole reason the bear had followed him was out of curiosity. But he was foremost a realist, and his practical nature balked at the flight of fancy.

Zach and Shakespeare spent the ride back debating how best to go about snuffing the bear's life. Zach was all for tracking it to its lair and disposing of it with well-placed shots. But Shakespeare pointed out that to go after the bear in the forest was to wage the fight on the bear's terms.

"How else, then?" Zach asked.

"We make it come to us," Shakespeare suggested. "We set out bait to bring it into the open."

Winona and Evelyn were waiting outside the cabin, Winona with an upraised lantern. "It got away?" she said in a tone of deep regret. "We have not seen the last of it, I am afraid."

"There's a good chance it won't bother us," Nate said, but even he did not believe his statement.

Winona mustered smiles for Zach and McNair. "We are about to sit down to supper. You are welcome to join us."

"I am flattered, fair lady," Shakespeare responded in his grandiloquent way, "but with that monster lurking about, I must hie me to my own fair maiden and stay by her side."

"Same here, Ma," Zach said.

Shakespeare lifted his reins. "Before we depart, let's make a pact. Should any of us hear gunshots, we will rush to the aid of whoever the bear has attacked. Agreed?"

Zach nodded. "Fine by me."

"The griz probably won't show its face," Nate said, "but as a precaution it can't hurt."

A sudden gust of wind caused Shakespeare to twist in his saddle and face to the west. He sniffed a few times, then said, "There is a storm on the way. It will hit before midnight, unless I miss my guess."

Nate glanced skyward, where nary a cloud marred the blue. Long ago he had learned not to question his friend's uncanny ability to predict changes in the weather. McNair had lived in the Rockies so long, he was extremely sensitive to their many tempers. "More cause for us not to worry," Nate mentioned. "Bears don't like to be out in the rain any more than we do."

"Some people, and some silver-tips, don't care one whit whether they get wet or not," Shakespeare said. "Keep your wits about you, and your eyes and ears skinned. Remember, in the dark the griz has all the advantages."

"You're scaring me, Uncle Shakespeare," Evelyn said.

"Good. There's nothing like a little fear, girl, to keep

a person on their toes." The craggy-visaged frontiersman grinned and winked, and lashed his mare.

"My turn," Zach said. But he paused to say to Nate,
"Don't let your feelings get in the way of your common
sense, Pa."

"How's that again?"

"I know you. I know how you think. You want to
spare that bear so you will go out of your way not to
harm it if you can. But please, for all our sakes, if you
have the chance, blow out its wick."

"What do you take me for?" Nate was a trifle indig-
nant. "I would never let my personal sentiments put
any of you in danger."

"I'm glad to hear that." Zach nodded at each of them
in turn, then headed north along the shore at a gallop.

For a minute no one spoke or moved. Nate gazed toward the forest, now an inky silhouette against the
backdrop of descending night.

"Brrrrrrrr," Evelyn said, shivering. "The wind sure is
cold. Do you reckon maybe winter will come early this
year?"

"We will not see snow for a moon or two yet,"
Winona said, draping an arm about her daughter's
shoulders. "Inside with you. Supper is ready, remember?" She beckoned to Nate. "You too, husband."

"I need to put my horse in the corral first," Nate said.
He did so, shut the gate, fastened the rawhide loop, and
patted one of the thick rails. They were sturdy enough,
but he was under no illusions; he had witnessed the immense strength grizzlies possessed. None of the horses
betrayed any alarm, though, as they were bound to if
they caught its scent. The bay came over and he patted
its neck. "Let's hope that griz learned something today."

133

The wind had picked up. Clouds were scuttling in over the western peaks like giant ethereal crabs, and far in the distance the sky lit with flashes of lightning.

"Just what we need," Nate said. "A thunderstorm." He gave the benighted woodland a last scrutiny, then went inside, making it a point to bar the door.

Winona was at the fireplace, bent over a black pot, stirring stew with a large wooden spoon. The room was warm and cozy, a startling contrast to the tempest brewing outside.

Nate leaned his Hawken against the wall and took his accustomed place at one end of the table. "I'm hungry enough to eat a gallon all by my lonesome," he remarked, patting his stomach.

"I made plenty," Winona said.

Evelyn brought bowls from the cupboard. Winona ladled stew into them, and they carried the bowls to the table.

The aroma set Nate's stomach to growling. "Told you I was famished," he said with a grin. "Is that rabbit I smell?"

"You have a good nose, husband," Winona said. "It came out of the woods this afternoon, and you know how much I like rabbit meat."

"Ma has shot more rabbits than you have grizzlies," Evelyn said. "Maybe we should change her name to Rabbit Killer."

Nate chuckled much louder than the jest called for. "And we should change your name from Blue Flower to Never Makes Her Bed Up."

"That's not fair. I do it now and then."

Their mood lightened, and during supper they chatted about the kind of things they normally would; how well the small garden Winona had planted was doing, how well Evelyn was applying herself to her studies, and speculation on when Zach and Louisa would become parents.

Now that the new cabins were built and everyone was settled in, Louisa was keenly desirous to have their first child. Nate had been there when she broke the news, and had noticed that his son did not greet it with equal enthusiasm. Thinking back, he seemed to recollect that while he had been excited at the prospect of his own firstborn, his excitement had been dampened by anxiety. He had not felt ready to be a father, and fretted that he would make a mess of it.

"Blue Water Woman was telling me—" Winona began, but stopped when a gust of wind howled like a demented wolf and shook the deerskin flap that covered the window.

Nate gazed apprehensively at that flap. It would be months before the glass pane he had ordered at Bent's Fort arrived. The window was not large enough for the bear to squeeze through, but it still made Nate uneasy.

"As I was saying," Winona resumed, "Blue Water Woman says she saw a giant fish the other day. It was swimming near her cabin, in shallow water."

"How giant, Ma?" Evelyn asked.

"As big as your father."

"Maybe it's the one that has been making the waves," Evelyn said. "What kind was it?"

"Blue Water Woman did not know. She did not get a good look at it," Winona answered.

"If it was as big as she claimed," Nate said, "it has to be a catfish or a sturgeon." Both grew to great lengths. But catfish were not found that high up in the mountains, and the only lake in the mountains to contain sturgeon, to the best of his knowledge, was the one now called Flathead Lake by the whites, which was many miles to the north.

"We must be on the watch when we bathe or swim," Winona said. "The old ones of my people say that big fish will sometimes pull people under and eat them."

"That's what whites call a folk tale," Nate said. "We have the same silly superstition east of the Mississippi."

"That story you read to me about a headless horseman is a folk tale," Winona responded. "Believing that an animal that eats whatever it can catch will eat people if it can catch them is not."

"I'll never set a toe in our lake again," Evelyn vowed. "That one, or any other."

"Nonsense," Nate scuffed. "When was the last time you heard of anyone being dragged under?"

"My people have stories of it happening," Winona said. "It is why some lakes are bad medicine, and we avoid them."

"None of those accounts are about our lake," Nate reminded her, peeved she was feeding Evelyn's fear. "We're perfectly safe."

"Except for the grizzly and the mountain lions and the wolverines and the wolves and the rattlesnakes," Evelyn said, "and any hostiles or renegade whites who happen by."

"The grizzly won't bother us," Nate stubbornly asserted.

No sooner were the words uttered than a commotion broke out in the corral. Several of the horses whinnied stridently, and there was a loud *thud* against the side of the cabin.

Nate was out of his chair before the whinnies died. Scooping up his Hawken, he lifted the heavy bar, set it aside, and said over his shoulder, "Bar the door behind me just in case."

Full night claimed the valley, the darkness compounded by a low blanket of clouds that plunged the cabin and its surroundings in a blackness as dark as that at the bottom of a well. Pitch blackness that Nate's eyes could scarcely penetrate more than a yard or two. He drew up short, the hair on his neck prickling, as a pungent scent tingled his nostrils. It was a scent he had smelled before, most noticeably the time he had poked his head inside a bear den.

Backing up until his back brushed the cabin, Nate sidled toward the corral. The horses were in a frenzy of excitement, raising a ruckus with their prancing and nickering.

Nate wished he had brought the lantern.

As if in answer, light spilled from the doorway and out came Winona, her rifle in one arm, the lantern held aloft. "Husband?"

"I told you to bar the door."

Winona sidestepped toward him. "Since when does a woman listen to her man?" she tried to make light of the situation. "And I saw you had forgotten this." She wagged the lantern.

"You should not leave Evelyn alone."

"It would be worse to let you face the grizzly alone," Winona said. "Or have you also forgotten I am your wife, and Shoshone women always stand by their husbands?"

Nate could not stay angry. "Have I mentioned lately how much I love you?"

"Reminders are always welcome," Winona said cheerfully, but there was nothing cheerful about the grim set of her jaw or the wary cast to her eyes. "It is here."

"I know." Nate touched her arm, then stalked to the corner. Most of the horses were milling nervously about. A few, the bay included, had stopped and were staring into the night to the northwest. He gazed in the same direction but saw nothing other than the blackness. "I should go for a look-see."

"You should do no such thing," Winona disagreed. "In the dark you can not see as well as it can, and with this wind, you would not hear it."

Nate tilted his head. She had a point about the wind. It was shrieking out of the mountains like so many banshees, a harbinger of the tempest soon to be unleashed. Already tiny wet droplets moistened his cheeks and forehead.

The wind suddenly whipped the lantern, and Winona nearly dropped it. Thrusting her rifle at Nate, she gripped the lantern's handle with both hands and held it close to the wall so it was shielded by their bodies, then reclaimed her Hawken. "We should go back in."

Nate balked. He did not like leaving the horses untended.

A cold drizzle started to fall. The lantern's glow was reduced by half. Worse, the rain further smothered sounds.

"Lead the way," Nate said into his wife's ear, and covered her as she hastened to the door, and knocked.

Evelyn had to remove the bar to admit them. "Did you see anything?" she anxiously asked.

"No," Nate said, which was the truth as far as it

went. "Let's finish eating." He sat and dipped his spoon into the bowl, but he had lost his appetite. After a few spoonfuls he set it down and announced, "I'll eat later." Rising, he carried the Hawken to the window. The deerskin was stretched taut and tied at all four corners to pegs in the jamb, and to two additional pegs midway down. The wind whistled past the edge, but so far no rain had got in.

A bright flare briefly lit the flap, followed by a clap of thunder that rumbled across the valley.

Neither Winona nor Evelyn were eating. They had their spoons poised over their bowls and were listening to nature's tantrum.

"I always liked the rain when I was little," Evelyn commented. "Not so much anymore."

The horses had quieted. Nate put an ear to the flap to be sure and thought he heard a suggestion of heaving breathing. Quickly he pried at the edge of the hide and peeked out but the bear was not there.

"One of us could climb on the roof," Winona recommended.

In the spring and summer, Nate often did just that. He would lie on his back for hours admiring the stars and contemplating the immensity of creation. As Shakespeare liked to say, there was nothing like a starry night to make a man appreciate how minuscule he was. "We couldn't see much from up there. The horses will just have to get by on their own."

More lightning lit the flap. More thunder boomed. The drizzle became a downpour, the drops pattering the cabin like a thousand tiny hammers.

"This would be a nice night to sleep if not for the griz," Evelyn commented.

139

Nate leaned his shoulder against the jamb. It was strange, he reflected, how the skein of his life had been interwoven with those of the lords of the mountains. That first grizzly he slew way back when, a fluke if ever there was one, had resulted in a warrior bestowing the name Grizzly Killer on him. A name Indians respected, for to kill a grizzly was accounted a great feat worthy of the bravest and strongest. After he slew several more, again not by choice but circumstance, even his fellow trappers regarded him with awe and respect. His story was told and retold around campfire after campfire, until he found himself, amazingly enough, regarded as highly as Shakespeare, Bridger, Walker and the like, on the white side, and as one of the mightiest of hunters by the red man.

All because he happened by mere chance to stab a grizzly in the eye as it was about to devour him.

"Did you hear that, Pa?" Evelyn intruded on his reverie.

Nate snapped his head up. From the vicinity of the corral came a sound muffled by the din of the elements. He could not quite identify it. But the next sounds he certainly could: a piercing whinny, punctuated by a roar that drowned out the rain and the wind, and a tremendous crash.

"It is after the horses!" Winona cried.

Nate sprang to the door.

Chapter Nine

Fierce wind buffeted Nate and cold rain lashed his face as he ran to the north end of the cabin and raised his Hawken. Continual bolts of lightning lit the sky in brilliant flashes, revealing the scene before him in all its grisly horror.

A section of the corral had been smashed to kindling. Thick rails had been shattered like twigs and left lying in pieces on the ground. In the center of the corral two horses were down in spreading pools of red. One was still but the other was feebly kicking and neighing.

For an instant Nate thought it was his bay, and he fought down an impulse to shriek in fury. Bounding past the broken rails, he saw that both animals were packhorses. The dead one had its neck ripped wide, strips of flesh hanging in shreds, flayed by claws that could rend like razors. The other horse had been disemboweled and lay amid its organs, including thick coils of intestines.

The rest of the horses were gone, fled into the night. Nor was there any sign of the grizzly.

A glow bathed Nate, casting his shadow on the gore-spattered ground. Blinking water from his eyes, he turned.

Winona and Evelyn had followed him, each with their rifles, Winona with the lantern over her head. The wind whipped it, threatening to tear it from her grasp, as she bent forward to better view the carnage.

Evelyn gasped.

"Back inside!" Nate hollered to be heard above the upheaval. "Bar the door and don't open it unless I knock!"

Winona rose on her toes toward his ear. "We are in this together, husband. We will stay with you."

"Don't argue," Nate said, his skin crawling as he peered into the driving wall of rain. The grizzly could be only a few yards away and they would not know it. "For Evelyn's sake, if not your own."

Frowning, Winona glanced at their daughter, then nudged Evelyn's arm and hurried toward the door.

Nate backed after them. The door slammed, and he heard the bar thump home. With his back to the wall and thunder resounding in his ears, he debated whether to go after the bear or wait for it to come to him.

Yet another spear of lightning was hurled to earth. It struck a tall pine near the edge of the trees with a crackling crash. The pine instantly erupted into flames that the deluge instantly smothered. But in the few brief moments of the flash and the flames, a huge form was silhouetted against the night, not twenty feet from the cabin.

Nate took a hasty bead but a veil of darkness descended. At the next bolt he tensed to shoot but the grizzly was no longer there. He looked right and left, but it was as if the ground had opened up and swallowed it.

Nate's mouth had gone completely dry. He tried to swallow and couldn't. It was easily remedied by opening his mouth and raising his face into the pelting rain. He blinked again to clear his vision.

Without warning a giant four-legged shape hove out of the storm nearly on top of him. Nate had not heard it. He went to thumb back the hammer, then recognized it for what it was: one of their packhorses, a favorite of his, a piebald as gentle and manageable as a lamb. He reached for it.

From out of the downpour hurtled a living embodiment of predatory bloodlust. With a roar that froze the piebald in terror, the grizzly was on the hapless horse in the blink of an eye. Teeth as long as Nate's fingers ripped into its neck and shoulder. Claws even longer shredded flesh to the bone.

The piebald squealed as it went down.

Nate aimed and fired but instead of the blast of a shot and the billow of gunsmoke, there was a *click*.

The grizzly was tearing into the piebald in a bestial rage. Hide and flesh flew every which way.

Dropping his right hand to a flintlock, Nate drew the pistol and cocked it. The bear was only ten feet away. The ball might have an effect. He fired. But as his finger was tightening, a square of light washed over him and hands grabbed the back of his buckskin shirt and he was bodily jerked backward into the cabin.

The door slammed shut. Winona and Evelyn barred it, Winona saying, "We heard the thing husband, and I looked out and saw you."

Only then did Nate realize the window flap was partly undone, the loose corner flapping wildly.

"What happened?" Winona asked.

"Misfire." Nate set the Hawken and the pistol on the table. Since not enough rain had seeped down the rifle's barrel to foul the powder, it had to be something else. He was bending to examine the hammer and the pan when out of the corner of his eye he glimpsed Evelyn, retying the flap. A premonition stabbed through him, an awful, terrible certainty, and he started to turn to shout for her to get away from the window. But the premonition came too late.

The flap seemed to explode inward. One instant it was intact, the next the grizzly's head was thrust inside, its rending teeth reducing the rawhide flap to strips and bits.

Nate's blood froze in his veins. He heard Evelyn scream as she flung herself away from the beast's wide maw, which was about to enfold her.

Then Winona was there. Seizing Evelyn by the shoulders, Winona pulled her beyond reach of the grizzly's gnashing teeth. They fell to the floor, Winona clasping Evelyn to her, as the bear roared in foiled frustration.

Nate drew his other pistol. The bear was clawing at the window in a frenzied attempt to force its way inside. He aimed squarely at the great head, and fired. At that range he could not miss. The ball struck the grizzly squarely between the eyes and dug a furrow in its fur but glanced off its thick skull and imbedded itself in the jamb.

All that achieved was to make the grizzly madder.

Nate bent to the Hawken. Only the rifle would slay the brute. But before he could make sure it would fire, a sharp *crack* resounded. The window was giving way under the grizzly's immense power and weight. Unless he did something, and quickly, the bear would soon be inside.

Nate drew his tomahawk and his Bowie knife. Under ordinary circumstances he would not think of doing what he was about to do. But it was not as futile as it seemed. The bear had not been able to force its forepaws through the opening, so all Nate had to contend with were its teeth. His wife and daughter were scrambling to their feet as he launched himself at the grizzly's head.

"No!" Winona cried.

Nate swung the tomahawk with all his might. The edge bit deep into fur and bone above the grizzly's left eye, and blood spurted. Its next roar shook the cabin. Nate sprang back as iron jaws snapped at his torso, losing a few whangs off his sleeve.

"Pa! Get back!"

Nate leaped in close, swinging both weapons, and connected. But the wounds he inflicted were superficial. Neither the tomahawk nor the Bowie could cleave through inches-thick bone to the bear's brain. Its teeth, on the other hand, could shear through him like daggers through wax. A quick twist saved him. He swung at an eye and again hit bone.

"I need a clear shot!" Winona yelled, her rifle wedged to her shoulder. "Move, husband! Move!"

Nate dived for the floor. There was the blast, and a roar, and he glanced up to see the window empty save for the tattered flap. Elated, he leaped to the sill, shoulder-to-shoulder with Winona. But the grizzly was not lying dead outside. It was gone.

"Did I hit it?" Winona wondered.

"You had to," Nate said. Yet if she had there should be blood, even if only a few drops, either on the sill or the ground. The rain could not have washed it away in the seconds it took them to reach the window.

Suddenly the south wall of the cabin vibrated to a heavy thump. Nate and Winona straightened and spun, Winona's fingers flying as she reloaded. Nate ran to the table, and his Hawken.

The blow was repeated a few yards to the left.

"It's trying to break in!" Evelyn exclaimed.

"Let it!" Nate had complete confidence in his craftsmanship. He had built the walls to withstand the worst that could be dished out by man, beast, or the elements. The logs were so thick that he had to rig a hoist to lift them into place. A man with an ax would need a good half an hour to chop through; the bear would take twice that. The only weak spots were the window and the door.

The thumps continued, as regular as the ticking of a clock. The grizzly rounded the southeast corner and pounded on the rear wall, going its entire length. All it did was loosen some chinking. It came to the northeast corner, and the other side of the corral. A splintering noise told Nate that the rails there had suffered the same fate as the rails at the front.

Struggling to contain her fear, Evelyn asked, "Should we run for it? To Zach's or Uncle Shakespeare's?"

Winona glanced at Nate. "We might make it in this storm."

They might. The rain and the wind would erase their tracks and their scent. But Nate did not relish being out in the open with that monster. Another misfire could prove fatal. "We are safer here."

Evelyn bit her lower lip and fidgeted. "I don't like being boxed in. I'd rather take my chances outside."

"Too risky," Nate said. The cabin walls were the only thing standing between them and annihilation.

Winona opened her mouth as if to argue but closed it again, and nodded. "Your father is right, Blue Flower. As hard as it is on your nerves, you must be patient. Eventually the bear will lose interest and leave."

"You hope," Evelyn said.

As if to prove Winona wrong, the pounding began anew on the north wall. Blows so powerful, the wall shook as in an earthquake. Dust filled the air, and Evelyn broke into a coughing fit.

Apparently the grizzly heard her. It delivered the most powerful blow yet, and its roar bid nigh to shatter their eardrums.

"How much more of this must we take?" Evelyn asked, more to herself than to them.

"It will soon be over," Winona assured her, but her tone lacked conviction.

By now the grizzly had reached the northwest corner and was only six or seven feet from the window.

Nate put a finger to his lips, then motioned for his wife and daughter to stay right where they were. Crouching, he crept near to the rain-lashed tatters of the flap, but not so near that the rain could drench his rifle. He aimed at the center of the window, ready to fire the split second the brute's huge head appeared. But all that came through the window was more rain and gusts of shrieking wind.

The pounded had ceased. The bear had tired of trying to batter in the walls. Now what would it do? Nate wondered, and had his answer the very next moment when the door was struck by a fur-covered battering ram.

Nate swivelled on the balls of his moccasins. *The grizzly had swung wide of the window and by accident—or was it crafty bestial design?—was assaulting the one point at which it might actually force entry*. The door was struck a second time, causing the bar to jump in its braces.

Evelyn screamed. Her hand to her throat, raw panic twisted her young features.

Dashing over, Winona clasped her daughter and said in her ear, "Calm yourself, Blue Flower. A Shoshone must not show fear even when she is afraid."

"But I'm only part Sho—" Evelyn began, and catching herself, closed her eyes and breathed into her mother's buckskin dress, "I'm sorry, Ma. I'll do my best."

Nate, meanwhile, sidestepped to the left until he was directly in front of the door. He did not like the idea of putting holes in it after all the time and work he had invested in hewing and planing the planks, but he fixed the Hawken's sights two inches above the bar, in the very center, and held his breath to steady his aim. He did not need to hold it long.

Roaring hideously, the grizzly slammed into the door yet again.

Nate fired. His Hawken was .60-caliber, large enough to bring down any game on the continent if the shot was well placed. It had a 34-inch octagonal barrel, a crescent butt plate, and unlike his pistols, a percussion lock. It was a work of art as much as a tool, and it, and its predecessors, had served him in excellent stead more times than he would ever care to count.

The Hawken did not fail him now. The ball cored through the door as neatly as a drill, and from the other side issued a savage snarl that ended in a gurgling grunt.

"You hit it, Pa!" Evelyn cried.

Nate thought so, too, but he never took anything for granted. He began reloading. First he poured powder down the muzzle, then he tamped a ball and patch on top of the powder using the ramrod housed under the barrel. He always cut his own patches, and always kept a score or so in his ammo pouch, along with plenty of percussion caps.

Outside, all was quiet. So quiet, Nate heard rain pattering the roof, and a soft sigh of relief from his daughter.

"Do you reckon it has left?"

"Could be," Nate said, but he was not venturing from the cabin until daylight, even if the storm stopped before then. "You two try to get some sleep."

"You must be joshing, Pa."

"I could not sleep if my life depended on it," Winona remarked. "You can try if you want, husband. We will take turns standing watch."

Nate agreed to take the first turn. Roosting in a chair with his feet propped on the table, he rested the

Hawken across his lap and folded his hands on top of it. A sharp blast of wind made him regret not keeping a spare window flap handy for emergencies. Live and learn, he reflected. Tomorrow he would remedy his oversight.

Winona was moving toward the window with a blanket in one hand and a hammer and nails in the other.

"What do you think you are doing?" Nate brought her up short.

"What does it look like? We can't leave it uncovered all night."

"Sure we can." In Nate's mind's eye, he envisioned a rain-soaked paw sweeping in to clutch Winona and pull her from the cabin. "A little moisture never hurt anyone. We'll do that after the sun comes up."

"But the floor is getting wet."

"I can always replace a few warped boards," Nate said. "I can't replace you."

Winona smiled and came over and kissed him on the cheek. "You can be so adorable."

"Get to sleep, wench," Nate said gruffly, and gave her fanny a playful light swat. "I'll wake you when it is your turn."

Pretending to be scandalized, Winona took a step back in mock shock. "Are all white men so brazen?"

They laughed, but their attempt to lighten the mood was not appreciated by everyone.

"How can you two fool around at a time like this?" Evelyn asked in amazement. "We could have been killed just now."

"Life is a lot more bearable when you learn to laugh at it," Nate responded, and was puzzled when his daughter groaned. "What's the matter? Are you feeling poorly?"

"Did you really just say 'bearable'?"

Nate blinked, and laughed some more. "I guess I did, didn't I? I believe that is called a pun, in case you didn't know."

"Please spare us from any more," Evelyn joined in the spirit of their forced frivolity.

Winona touched Nate's cheek. "You really should sleep first. You need the rest more than me. You were up in the mountains all day."

Nate insisted she turn in, with a furtive bob of his head at their daughter. Evelyn was the one they should be thinking of, and Winona was better at inducing her to get to sleep.

So it was that in a very short while, mother and child were curled up in blankets side-by-side in front of the softly crackling fireplace, while Nate sat at the table listening to them whisper to one another. Thanks to the wind and the rain he could hear little of what was being said, but that was all right. The important thing was that Winona would soon have Evelyn deep in dreamland.

Minutes dragged past, weighted by anchors. Nate prayed to the Almighty that they had seen the last of the bear that night, but there was no predicting bear behavior. Maybe it would stay away and maybe it would return. His skin crawled at any and all sounds he could not identify. Fortunately they were few. Once, about half an hour after the others had turned in, he thought he heard heavy breathing from close outside the window, but when he cocked his head, the sound faded. He chalked it up to overwrought nerves.

One thing was for sure. Nate had made a mistake in trying to train the grizzly to leave them be. His efforts had brought the beast down to the valley floor, and now he had no recourse but to do to this bear as he had done to so many others. He must slay it. He must hunt it down as soon as the sun rose.

Nate had seldom looked forward to a sunset so earnestly. He was sure that with the dawn the bear would vanish, and he could rest easy where his family was concerned. He thought of his son and his best friend, so near and yet so far, unaware of the nightmare being played out at his cabin. The thunder and driving rain had drowned out the shots and the roars. He considered firing into the air once the storm ended, but Zach and Shakespeare still might not hear if they were asleep, and the shots were bound to wake up Evelyn.

Nate idly glanced toward the fireplace, and smiled. They were both asleep, daughter and mother, Winona with an arm draped across Evelyn's shoulders. In the rosy glow of the fire their features were positively beautiful. He felt a rush of overwhelming love, love so deep and so intense, it brought an ache to his chest. They were literally and truly everything to him, two of the three people he loved most in the world. Two who, along with his son, were the more special because they were as much a part of him as his heart, and his lungs and his very breath.

Nate's gaze dwelled on Winona's angelic face. Incredible, he reflected, that he should love her as much now as he had back in the first flush of youthful passion. No, that was not entirely true, he realized; he loved her more. The years had enriched their caring for one another to where their two hearts were forever entwined. Two made one.

Nate had sometimes wondered what his life would have been like had he not met her. Frankly, he could not conceive of any other path. She meant that much to him. Without her—the very notion made him shudder.

Love was strange. It snuck up on a man like a thief in the night and stole all that he was and entrusted it into the safekeeping of someone else.

Love was wonderful. No other emotion produced so much happiness. No other emotion instilled so much joy. When Nate thought of all the happy moments he had shared with Winona, it filled him with a warmth that was warmer than any fire could ever impart.

Love was bewildering. Trying to define it was like trying to define an elusive will-o'-the-wisp. For it was always more than words could describe. To say that love was the binding of two souls was all well and good, but how exactly was that brought about? By what magic alchemy was the binding achieved? What made love so much more potent than any other emotion? And so much more long lasting? If the wisest minds humanity had to offer were right, love endured for all eternity. But how could anything endure an endless span? What was it about love that—

Nate stiffened in his chair. He heard the breathing again, from near the window. There could be no mistake this time. It was not his imagination. It was not stray puffs of wind.

The grizzly was back.

Lowering his moccasins to the floor, Nate gripped the Hawken in both hands and brought the stock to his shoulder. He would aim for the bear's eyes. With any luck, the ball would penetrate to the monster's brainpan. Or he might partially blind it, in which case finishing it off would be that much simpler.

The heavy breathing ended as abruptly as it had started.

Nate listened for footfalls but lightning and thunder were again waging war with the earth, and the banshees were at their infernal shrieking. He stared intently at the window but all he saw were sheets of rain, and the dark, as impenetrable as a wall.

The grizzly must be circling the cabin and waiting for an opportunity to strike.

A vague feeling of unease came over Nate. A feeling that grew stronger and stronger until he could not shrug it off as his imagination. A feeling that he was being watched. That even if he could not see the bear, the bear could see him.

Nate could not say what made him glance at the door. When he did, it took a few seconds for what he was seeing to register. In the center, above the bar, was the hole the heavy lead ball had made when he shot at the bear earlier. A hole about the size of a walnut. A hole that should be as empty as the window. But something was there. Something dark was pressed to the hole. Something dark, that glittered with the light of the fire, and with the flames of bestial hatred.

It was an eye.

Nate came out of the chair so fast, the chair nearly tipped over. He swung the Hawken toward the door but the eye disappeared. The tempest stilled for a few seconds, and in the momentary lull there came a growl. A growl that Nate would swear mocked him as a man might mock an adversary.

Nate's hands grew clammy with sweat. His breathing quickened. The eye had spooked him as nothing else could.

Suddenly the south wall creaked and seemed to bend slightly inward. Nate thought it was a trick of the firelight until he heard the scrape of claws on the logs. He moved toward the wall, puzzled, until it dawned on him what the grizzly was up to; the behemoth was trying to climb up on the roof.

Chapter Ten

Nate told himself that he must be mistaken. That the grizzly would not possibly try to gain the roof. That even if it did, it was too big and too heavy for its claws to support its immense weight. But the creaking grew louder and the wall shuddered as a man might shudder under a great burden.

Startled, Nate ran to the south wall and pressed an ear to a log. He heard a *scritch-scritch-scritch*, and more heavy breathing.

All bears could climb when they were young. Black bears, for the most part, could still climb as adults, although they were limited to the lower branches. Grizzlies became too massive for even the stoutest limbs, and once they were over a year old, climbing was no longer a pastime in which they could indulge.

But damn him, Nate thought, if it didn't sound as if the grizzly was slowly but laboriously doing the impossible! Consternation gripped him. What could the thing hope to accomplish? he wondered. The roof was as solid as the walls. More so, since he had reinforced it with rafters to withstand the periodic heavy snows the Rockies were prone to in the winter. Snow as high as the cabin, the drifts even higher.

The *scritching* and the *scratching* grew louder, as if the grizzly were scrabbling for a paw hold. Nate almost laughed at the image, and the bear's stupidity.

Then two of the upper logs shook more violently than the rest as the chinking between them broke and fell in bits and pieces. The chinking was mainly clay, from a deposit not far from the lake, and more than sufficient to keep out heat and cold and to withstand heavy rains. But it was not proof against sharp claws, claws that now gouged and scraped at the opening they had made to make the opening wider.

This could not be happening, Nate told himself. Yet it was. More pieces fell, and before Nate's astounded gaze the claws held fast, enabling the bear to lift itself higher.

The whole wall quaked and again seemed to bend inward from the enormous mass applying pressure on the other side.

More *scritching* drew Nate's eyes to where the wall met the roof. The tips of the claws he could see were on a rear paw. The bear's forepaws were scrabbling for a hold on the roof so the bear could pull itself the rest of the way up.

Evelyn whimpered in her sleep.

Nate raised the Hawken but promptly lowered it again. The walls were too thick. He could not shoot through them as he had the door. He was no longer convinced the grizzly was going to all its trouble for nothing. He should have known not to underestimate it.

Mumbling in her sleep, Winona rolled over on her back.

What with the scratching and the grunting and the creak and groan of the logs and the rafters, Nate expected his wife and daughter to wake up any second. Whirling toward the door, he took several swift strides. He intended to run out and around to the corner and shoot the grizzly before it achieved its purpose. But as his hand fell on the latch, the entire cabin shuddered and the logs overhead moaned as if in pain.

The bear had done it!

Nate gaped in disbelief at dust falling from above, and listened with growing dread to the ponderous tread of the monster, audible between booms of thunder.

"What woke me, husband?" Winona had sat up and was glancing about in confusion. "What is going on?"

Nate pointed at the ceiling.

"I don't understand," Winona said. "What about the ceiling?" The center beam creaked, followed by a scraping sound, as of claws being rubbed along the roof, and Winona came up off the floor, her eyes saucers of incredulity. "Is that what I think it is?"

"The griz," Nate confirmed.

"But how—" Winona gasped as a new sound fell on their ears.

"It's trying to claws its way inside," Nate divined. Not that the bear would succeed. The roof was almost as thick as the walls. The thought jolted him. *Almost as thick!* For the truth was, he had used smaller logs for the roof than for the walls. It would not take the bear as long to rip through them as it would to tear through one

159

of the walls. But that was not what caught Nate's breath in his throat. It was the realization that the bear did not have to claw all the way through. Halfway would suffice to buckle the log under the bear's weight, and once one log was dislodged, the rest would be that much weaker.

Here Nate thought he had built so well, but never in his wildest dreams had he imagined anything like *this*.

Winona was fingering her rifle. "What will we do if it gets through?"

"Shoot it. What else?" Nate said. But if their first shots did not kill it, they would be at the mercy of a creature that had no mercy.

"Now is when we should run to Zach's or Shakespeare's," Winona proposed. "We need help, and there is Blue Flower to think of."

"We would be worse off out in the storm," Nate disagreed.

"But—" Again Winona stopped.

The entire cabin shook to a loud *thump*. Nearly every log, every rafter, creaked or shifted. The *thump* was repeated, with the same result.

"What in the world?" Winona whispered.

God help him, but Nate knew the answer. He knew, and with the knowledge came the horrific truth that no matter what they did, stay or flee, they were in extreme peril. "It's jumping up and down on its front legs." Over half a ton of sinew and bone, slamming down on the roof again and again and again. The rafters were strong but they could not endure that sort of pounding indefinitely. Sooner or later something had to give, and it would not be the bear.

"Ma? Pa? What's all the ruckus?" Evelyn sat up and tiredly rubbed her eyes. "What is all the racket?"

Winona ran to her and scooped Evelyn into her arms. "We are in trouble, Blue Flower. You must wake up, and keep your wits about you."

"Trouble?" Another *thump* goaded Evelyn into looking up. Her sleepiness evaporated like dew under a blazing sun and she gasped, "Is that the grizzly?"

"It's not a chickadee," Nate said. He was paying particular attention to the rafters. The beams were six inches by six inches, or as near to that as he had managed with the tools he had at hand. So long as they held, the cabin could withstand the bear's onslaught. But should they give out—he refused to contemplate the consequences.

"Shouldn't we get out of here before the roof comes down on our heads?" Evelyn urged.

"We're safer here than we would be outdoors," Nate maintained. But were they? The rafters were giving him cause to doubt. They sounded just like a person in the throes of agony.

Winona was moving toward the door, guiding Evelyn in front of her, both riveted to the roof and the continued fall of dust. "Please, husband. Let us leave now, while we still can."

"You're letting your fear get the better of you," Nate said, and had to struggle with his own rising sense of panic when hairline cracks appeared in one of the crossbeams. "It can't be!"

"Pa?" Evelyn said anxiously.

The blows were louder. Nate envisioned the grizzly rising partway onto its rear legs and then smashing its forepaws down, as tireless as a steam engine. The timbers reminded him of teeth gnashing together. Teeth on the verge of splintering.

"Husband?" Winona said worriedly. "I do not like this. I do not like this one bit."

Neither did Nate. If the inconceivable happened, if the timbers gave way, the roof would crash down on top of them, crushing them to pulp.

The crack in the crossbeam widened.

Evelyn was mesmerized in terrified fascination. When the same crossbeam bent down almost to the breaking point, she broke, instead. With a loud cry she darted to the door and grabbed the bar.

"No! Wait!" Nate said, expecting Winona to stop her, but apparently Winona expected him to, because the next moment the bar was on the floor and Evelyn had lifted the latch, and yanked.

"Daughter, no!" Winona cried.

A fierce gust of wind howled through the doorway, bringing with it a sheet of driving rain. Evelyn cast another glance up, grabbed her rifle from where she had leaned it against the wall, and bolted.

Nate was only a step behind his wife when Winona reached the threshold. He figured Evelyn would only go a couple steps and stop but she had disappeared into the maelstrom.

"Where?" Winona asked in dismay, turning this way and that.

Shouldering past, Nate ran a few yards. Within heartbeats he was completely drenched. Large, hard, cold drops battered him like so many stones. Lightning lanced the firmament and thunder rattled the foundations of the earth. Above all rose a tremendous roar, as if in defiance of all that was and all that lived.

Nate turned and beheld a scene out of an improbable nightmare lent bestial form and gut-wrenching substance.

On top of their cabin, the behemoth's whole outline was etched against another unearthly display of lightning. A silhouette splashed in ink. A monster such as men had feared since the dawn of time. A dreadnought with an unquenchable appetite for flesh. The king of carnivores, a lord of the mountainous domain over which its kind ruled. Living hairy death on four redwood legs, a threshing machine unparalleled in the annals of the world.

In that instant the grizzly seemed to transcend all it was. The bear was more than a bear. The predator was more than a predator. It was the embodiment of humankind's most primal fears, the incarnation of death. A creature so unbelievably massive, so incredibly formidable, as to give rise to the innermost fears of all that saw it. Destruction lent life for one purpose and one purpose only; to kill and go on killing for as long as breath animated its gigantic frame.

The grizzly was a slap in the face to all those who claimed the world was the cradle of love and peace. It was nature at nature's rawest. An ever-present promise of oblivion to those who stumbled into its path.

For the plain truth of life was that there were no guarantees. Men and women were born to die, and nowhere was it written that the interval between birth and death would be one of bliss. Nowhere was there a promise that men and women would go from cradle to grave in perfect peace.

Nature was a harsh mistress. The natural order of things was a cruel order. Rain fell on the just and the unjust, just as grizzlies cared not one whit whether the person they slew was good or evil. They were as impersonal as nature itself. They were not there to judge, but to devour.

The bear was still slamming its front paws down on top of the cabin. It did not realize they were outside. But that changed when Winona cupped a hand to her mouth and shouted, "Blue Flower! Where are you!"

The grizzly looked down.

Nate's sole thought was to protect his family. He must save his wife and daughter by slaying the bear before it could reach them. Accordingly, he jerked the Hawken to his shoulder, thumbed back the hammer, aimed at the grizzly's chest, and fired.

Up on the roof, the grizzly rose onto its hind legs. Its rapier teeth gleamed in the glare of more lightning, and it uttered a roar that would chill most prey to the marrow. A roar of pain and unrivaled ferocity.

"There she is!" Winona suddenly cried, and raced into the rain.

Nate still had his eyes on the bear. He glimpsed his wife's flying figure and ran after her. He needed to reload, but he must stop and hunker so as not to get the powder wet, and he refused to stop until he caught up with Winona and Evelyn. He had gone twenty-five feet or so when he was appalled to discover he had gone the wrong way. He had no idea where they were. Casting wildly about in the hope of spotting them, he was facing the cabin when yet another vivid bolt cleaved the sky, briefly illuminating the roof.

The grizzly was no longer there.

Goose bumps broke out on Nate's skin. Not from the wet or the chill, but from the nerve-searing fact that the bear had climbed down and was hunting them. Dropping to his knees, he hunched forward so his back bore the brunt of the downpour, and began to reload. He had to be careful not to get the powder wet. In that he succeeded, but just as he was pouring the powder down the Hawken's muzzle, a blast of wind scattered half of it like so many grains of black sand.

Nate tried again, bending lower. He was listening for footsteps or any other indication the grizzly was close but the tempest denied him the luxury.

Then, from off to his right, there came a scream.

Nate's natural inclination was to rush to help. One of the hardest things he ever had to do was to fight the urge, to stay put for another thirty seconds to finish reloading. Heaving erect, he ran toward where he believed the scream came from. He shouted his wife's and daughter's names but it was doubtful either heard him above the damnable thunder. He stopped and tried to penetrate the rain but it was like peering into a waterfall. Water, water everywhere, with nary a clue as to the whereabouts of those who meant everything to him.

Furious, Nate shifted first one way and then another. "Winona! Evelyn! Where are you!" He did not care if the grizzly heard. In fact, he hoped it did. He would rather the bear came after him than after them, and if it did, he would put another ball into the brute and maybe end their ordeal.

An ominous growl warned he was getting his wish.

Nate spun, but the bear was not where he thought it would be. He hoped the relentless rain was dulling its senses as much as the rain baffled his own. He took a few steps, turned a different direction, and took a few more. But he saw nothing: not his wife, not his daughter, not the behemoth out to rend their flesh from their bones. "Where *are* you?" he said aloud to himself.

Lashed mercilessly by the downpour, Nate covered a couple yards when an indistinct shape gave him pause. Something was up ahead. Something big. But he could not tell if it was the bear or one of their horses. "Is that you, you hairy devil?" he hollered to provoke a growl, but the thing just stood there.

Nate warily advanced. A part of his mind screamed at him to run, but he had Winona and Evelyn to think of. He would gladly sacrifice his life to save theirs. All he asked was that he take the grizzly with him.

Whatever it was, the thing abruptly vanished. One instant it was there, the next it was swallowed by the deluge. He chased after it but the storm made a mockery of the attempt.

Nate tried to gauge where he was. He believed he was north of the cabin, nearer the lake than the forest. Beyond that, he could not hazard a guess.

A yell wavered on the wind. Nate spun, hope springing anew, but whether it came from south or west of him was impossible to say. He waited for the cry to be repeated. If it was, he never heard it.

Water cascaded down Nate's chest and back. Water plastered his hair to his head, his beard to his chin. He was so soaked, he was even wet between his toes. So soaked, his moccasins squished when he walked.

Nate debated his next move. He doubted Winona or Evelyn had returned to the cabin. More than likely, Evelyn had headed for Zach's place. Shakespeare's cabin was closer but Evelyn's affection for her brother would bend her steps to Zach's. Winona would do the same for the same reason he now did.

The crash of roiling surf told Nate just how close to the lake he had strayed. Shielding his eyes from the rain, he beheld a spectacle the likes of which he would never forget.

The storm had transformed the lake from a tranquil mirror of serenity into a raging Charybdis. Waves rose five and six feet high in unending succession. Were a canoe to be launched, it would be smashed to kindling.

Nate hurried on but had only gone a short distance when he saw an object that he thought *was* a canoe. One that had overturned and was lodged half-submerged near shore, with wave after wave pounding it.

Nate halted in surprise. He did not own a canoe. Nor did his son or McNair. Which meant it had to be an Indian canoe. But where were the Indians? More to the point, who were they? A tribe he was familiar with? The canoe might provide a clue. No two tribes constructed their canoes exactly alike. He moved toward it. Examining it would only take a few seconds. He came to the lake's storm-tossed edge, and waded in. The water rose as high as his ankle, then halfway to his knees. He was ten feet from the object when the remarkable occurred; the object rolled and then surged toward deeper water under its own power.

Flabbergasted, Nate watched whatever it was plow through the incoming waves with an ease that suggested considerable size and strength. He did not see fins, nor any suggestion of scales, but it had to be a fish, the largest he ever came across. If not for the storm he would have waded after it for a closer look. But all he could do was stand and watch until it arched its back and dived.

"I'll be damned," Nate said aloud. He remembered the women saying they had seen something strange in the lake, and Evelyn insisting the lake harbored a monster. But the only true monster in the valley was a land animal with iron jaws and a pronounced hump, and it was stalking them at that very moment.

Turning, Nate tucked his chin to his chest and thrust his shoulder into the wind. It was like being pushed by an invisible hand. He was almost out of the water when instinct prompted him to glance up. It was well he did.

The grizzly had found him. It had snuck up as silently as a ghost and was waiting for him to reach land. No warning growl or enraged roar issued from its furry throat. It waited in silent earnest to kill him.

Not if Nate could help it. He fired from the hip at the center of the bear's body and was rewarded with an explosion of movement as the griz hurtled right for him. Incredibly, the bear stopped when an incoming wave washed over its front paws. Instantly drawing a pistol, Nate fired again. He aimed at the neck and thought he saw blood fly but it might have been a spray of water.

The grizzly ended its silence with a roar to eclipse all roars. It reared onto its hind legs, its mouth yawned wide.

Nate shoved the spent flintlock under his belt and drew the other. This time he took deliberate aim. He must not miss. He must strike a vital organ or a vital vein or he was in for as grisly an end as any man ever had. But just as his trigger finger tightened, the grizzly dropped onto all fours and a huge paw flashed out, striking the pistol and swatting it from his hand.

Nate thrust the Hawken at the bear's face but the grizzly swatted that, too, tearing it from his grasp as easily as Nate would swat a fork from a baby's. Backpedaling until the water was almost to his knees, Nate drew his Bowie and his tomahawk and tensed for the final charge. But nothing happened. The bear stood there and glowered, its lips curled from its teeth.

Nate glanced down. Bears generally had no compunctions about getting wet. He had seen many a black bear and many a grizzly fishing or frolicking in rivers and the like. But for some reason this particular grizzly refused to enter the lake.

"Come and get me!" Nate shouted, but all the grizzly did was snarl.

A wave smashed against Nate's legs, nearly pitching him toward the bear. Righting himself, he planted both feet and resisted repeated buffets. But he could not stay there forever. The waves and the cold would weaken him. He hefted the Bowie and the tomahawk. Ordinarily, he would merit them a match for any enemy, man or beast, but against a grizzly they were puny excuses for weapons, akin to the shepherd boy David challenging the giant warrior Goliath armed with nothing but a slingshot against Goliath's huge sword and shield.

Lightning crackled, lending the illusion that the grizzly's eyes danced with fire and imbuing the bear with a demonic aspect.

Nate knew what he had to do but he hesitated. Barring a miracle, the outcome was foreordained, and he had no hankering to die.

The grizzly commenced pacing back and forth, its great head swinging from side to side, its fiery eyes always fixed on him.

Unbidden memories flooded through Nate. Memories of his many close shaves, of the bears he had fought and the mountain lions he had vanquished. Of the warriors he had battled and the renegade whites who had tried to take his life. He never went looking for trouble. Trouble always came to him. Left on his own, he would be content to live in peace with all things. But his sentiment was not shared by the many meat eaters that called the wilderness home, or the many two-legged killers who delighted in snuffing out lives as they would snuff out candles.

Maybe Nate was getting old, but he was tired of the bloodletting. When he was young he was a lot like his son, and met every threat with violence. Now, he would rather avoid a threat than confront it. Unfortunately, the grizzly left him no choice.

Not that Nate blamed the bear. It was his fault. He had tried to teach it to stay away from humans and instead had drawn the bear to them as surely as if he had hung a freshly killed buck from a tree limb as bait.

"Please go," Nate said.

The grizzly growled and went on pacing.

Nate remembered the very first grizzly he killed, so long ago, in an unnamed river on the vast expanse of prairie. Now here he was, in a lake in the mountains, in the self-same situation. His life had come full circle. Maybe, he mused, it was meant to be like this. Maybe this was his end. If so, he would face it as he had faced all the other threats in his life.

"As God is my witness, I did not want this."

At that, the grizzly halted, then pushed up onto its back legs, towering like a tree into the night. Raising its forepaws on high, it roared the primeval challenge its kind had voiced since their dawning.

Nate's feet were growing numb from the cold water. His legs could no longer take the strain of resisting the waves. He had to act, and act now. "Yea, though I walk through the valley of the shadow of death, I will fear no evil," he quoted, gripping the hilt of the Bowie and the haft of the tomahawk more firmly. "For Thou art with me. Thy rod and Thy staff they comfort me."

With that, Nate charged out of the lake to meet his destiny.

Chapter Eleven

Nate's rush caught the grizzly by surprise. He reached the bear before it could drop onto all fours. Darting in close, he slashed the tomahawk across its belly, then leaped back to avoid claws that would have sheared his head from his neck.

Springing to the right, Nate speared the Bowie into the great hairy body under the grizzly's left foreleg. The blade met little resistance and sank to the hilt. Yanking it out, he avoided the bear's grasp, and crouched.

Roaring in pain and baffled rage, the grizzly lowered its forelegs to the ground. It could have killed Nate then and there with a single bound, but the two wounds Nate inflicted had given it pause, and instead of attacking, it regarded him intently.

Nate's sole hope of surviving depended on his ending the unequal battle quickly. He must press the bear for all he was worth. To that end, he feinted to the left, and when the bear snapped at him, he went right. He heard its teeth gnash empty air even as he sliced the tomahawk into its neck. Again he thrust the Bowie but this time the grizzly backed away with amazing alacrity for so enormous a creature.

The bear was mad, mad as only a grizzly could get. So mad at the new pain, it launched itself at him like an enraged buffalo; lowering its head, it was on him in a twinkling.

Nate dived to one side. He felt a sharp pang in his ribs and a tug on his buckskin shirt. Then he was on the rain-soaked ground and rolling on his shoulder up into a crouch. The bear's flank was in front of him; he stabbed it in the butt.

A snarl rasped from the grizzly's throat. With quick-silver speed it whipped around and swung a razor-tipped paw.

Barely a fraction to spare, Nate skipped backward. Again he felt a stinging pain, across his sternum, but the claws did not sink deep enough to cripple or kill, and so long as he was breathing and could move, he would keep on fighting. He buried the tomahawk in the paw, wrenched it out before the grizzly could retaliate, and skipped aside to gain room to move.

The bear was terrible to behold. Its eye were pools of hellfire. Accustomed to slaying most foes quickly, the tactics of the two-legged jackrabbit was confounding and confusing it. But it was still supremely confident in its size and its strength, and it brought both into play in another headlong hurtle.

Nate sought to dodge but his luck failed him. His left arm spiked with excruciating agony as the grizzly's teeth sank to the bone. Involuntarily, he arched his back and nearly screamed. Before the bear could clamp down harder and crush his forearm to ruin, he streaked the tomahawk in an arc at the grizzly's head. He struck blindly in a bid to get the bear to release him. By sheer happenstance, the tomahawk caught it full in its right eye.

Now it was the griz that opened its mouth wide in torment, and sprang away, shaking its great head in an attempt to clear its vision. But there was no clearing the sight of an eyeball sliced in twain. All the shaking accomplished was to dislodge part of the eye from its socket and leave it dangling like a dark pea at the end of a long stem.

Nate struggled to focus. The combined pain from his side, his chest and especially his arm threatened to black him out. Sudden weakness pervaded his limbs, and he backed way, his senses reeling. If the bear had attacked at that moment, it would have been over. But the bear continued to shake its head and snarl hideously, and in another few moments the deluge hid it from view.

Nate turned and ran. He had to get away before the bear recovered and came after him. He had no idea which direction he was going. He did not care. The important thing was to put distance between them, for as surely as the sun rose and set, the grizzly would be out to tear him into little pieces.

Nate was counting on the rain to mask his scent, but a grizzly's sense of smell was so uncannily sensitive, the barest trace might be enough to draw it like a magnet.

His arm was throbbing. Gritting his teeth, he moved

it up and down. It hurt like blazes but he could use it if he had to, and he would soon have to.

Nate's one consolation was that by now Winona and Evelyn must be halfway to Zach's. They were safe. No matter what befell him, they would live. Winona would avenge him. She would insist on tracking the bear down and slaying it, and Zach and Shakespeare would help her. They would all get on with their lives, and hopefully live to ripe old ages. They—

Nate stopped dead. Something had risen out of the night to bar his way. Blinking against the rain, he slowly moved forward, than laughed at his foolishness. It wasn't the bear. It was the corral. He started to follow it around when a growl warned him the bear was stalking him. He considered running to the cabin but the grizzly might overtake him before he got there. Another growl, even louder, spurred him to desperation; hooking his good arm over the uppermost rail, he climbed up, turned, and balanced on the balls of his feet.

Not an instant too soon.

Out of the rain hove the grizzly, sniffing noisily and growling nonstop. It came so close to the corral that Nate could have reached out and touched its hump. But the grizzly did not spot him.

Nate almost let the bear go by. But it would only come back, or wander off into the night and live to wreak havoc another day. He could not permit that. He had the lives of those he loved to think of. If he could end it, he must try, no matter the potential consequences.

So it was that Nate uncoiled like a spring and launched himself into the air. Some people would call him insane but there was a rationale behind his madness. That rationale was to slay the bear by any means necessary.

Nate alighted on the grizzly's hump. Sprawling onto his belly, he instantly swung his legs over the bear's side while simultaneously sinking the Bowie its full length into the bear's flesh. In doing so, he unleashed an ursine whirlwind.

Roaring ferociously, the grizzly reared onto its hind legs and tried to claw Nate from his perch. But the grizzly's forelimbs were not long enough to reach him. So the bear twisted from side to side, seeking to throw him off.

With his legs clamped tight, Nate stayed on. He swung the tomahawk, slicing it deep into the hump.

Dropping on all fours, the grizzly bucked like a wild horse. For all its size, it could jump clear off the ground and arc its back into a bow. Each time it came down was like a blow to Nate's body. His left arm began to weaken. Suddenly the grizzly crashed into the correl, shattering several rails. A flying piece of pine tore a furrow across Nate's temple, deep enough that he bled.

All the while, the hard, cold rain fell, stinging Nate ceaselessly. He clung on, swinging the tomahawk again and again. Each blow heightened the bear's frenzy.

That was when the cabin materialized. Unable to stop, the bear crashed into the wall. Nate tried to lift his leg but he was a shade slow. Pain seared him like a red-hot poker. His hold on the Bowie slackened, and he was in danger of being thrown, How he clung on, he would never know, but he did, and the next he knew, the bear had barreled through a gap in the rails and was spinning and jumping like a dervish.

Nate drove the tomahawk deep into the bear's neck. He figured its wounds would weaken it but if its bucking was any indication, its stamina was limitless. He raised the tomahawk to do it again just as the grizzly whirled. Off he flew, losing his hold on the Bowie, and the bear.

Nate smashed onto the unyielding ground. Dazed, all he could do was lie there as the world blurred. He was easy prey if the bear decided to sink its teeth into his throat. But when he twisted his head and looked up, the grizzly was nowhere to be seen. Thinking it must be behind him, he rolled onto his back, but it was not there, either.

Nate painfully rose to his knees. It hurt to breathe. He suspected one or two of his ribs were cracked, if not broken. His side and his chest had stopped bleeding but not his arm. He held his wrist close to his face and winced at sight of the mangled flesh under the torn sleeve.

Resisting dizziness, Nate uncurled and moved toward a rectangle of light. At his first step his left leg nearly buckled. His ankle started throbbing. Somehow or other he had sprained it.

Nate willed his body forward. He was battered and bloody but he was not beaten. He kept expecting the grizzly to pounce but he came to the light without mishap. The cabin door was wide open. Flames still crackled in the hearth. Everything was exactly as they had left it except that now there was a wet half-moon on the floor inside the door as well as under the window.

Eagerly, Nate entered. He used his shoulder to push the door shut, then bent to lift the bar. The anguish provoked showed his left arm was not up to it. Leaving the bar where it was, he stepped to the table, placed the tomahawk on it, and sank into a chair. Exhaustion racked him. He needed to shed his wet clothes and bandage himself as best he could but he was too weak, too tired. All he wanted was to lie down and rest.

With a rare oath, Nate sat up straight. Thinking like that could get him killed. He must change clothes, yes, but then he must make sure Winona and Evelyn were all right.

Rising, Nate limped toward a closet where his spare buckskins hung. Opening it, he leaned against the wall to gird his strength, then tugged at his wet shirt to pull it over his head. The shirt was so wet, it stuck to him like wax. He could not peel it any higher than his chest.

Red drops fell from his arm to the floor. Nate decided to cut the shirt off so he could bandage his wrist. He had lost his Bowie but Winona kept a butcher knife and other implements in a counter drawer. Shambling over, he opened the drawer and had to move silverware to find the butcher knife.

Nate inserted the tip of the blade into his shirt and was about to cut upward when a familiar creak filled the cabin. Familiar because he had heard it many times before; it was the creak of leather hinges when the front door opened.

Fully aware what he would behold, Nate turned.

Death incarnate was framed in the doorway. Blood matted the grizzly's head and neck, and the one eye still dangled from its socket.

Nate sidled toward the table, and his tomahawk. He had an extra pistol, an older flintlock, in a chest in the same closet as his shirt, but fetching it and loading it would entail time the bear was not likely to grant.

Sure enough, the grizzly gave voice to another of its ear-shattering roars and threw itself through the doorway. Or tried to. The doorway was wide enough for humans, but not behemoths. Its front shoulders wedged fast, and try as it might, the grizzly could not force entry. Incensed beyond endurance, it bit and clawed and pushed and strained, all the while its eye flapped and swung madly about.

Nate reclaimed the tomahawk. By rights he should stay well back and only swing when it was safe, but something inside of him, something deep down in his being, snapped. He had tried to spare this bear, tried hard to preserve its life, and look at what had happened. All he wanted was for him and his to be left alone. Was that too much to ask? Anger boiled within him, a stepping-stone to pure and total fury.

"Back for more, are you, you bloodthirsty bastard?" Nate cried, and threw himself at his would-be destroyer.

The next moments were a blur. Nate slashed and stabbed like a madman gone amok. He saw the grizzly snap at his body, felt claws rake his arms and his legs. But he was past caring, past the pain and the weakness, past everything except the compulsion to kill, kill, kill. Thunder pulsed in his ears, but not the thunder of the tempest. It was his own blood, racing through his veins.

Teeth tore Nate's shoulder. Claws ripped his shin. But still he stood his ground and swung and screamed into the teeth-rimmed maw.

"Die, damn you! Die!"

Nate stabbed with the butcher knife, straight into the grizzly's other eye. A new sound burst from the lord of the mountains. Not a roar or a growl or a snarl, but a howl of pain and shock, and perhaps, just perhaps, a tinge of fear.

Suddenly surging backward, the grizzly broke free of the doorway and spun to run into the night.

Nate flew after it. He cut its rear leg, cut its side. The grizzly stopped and reared, its forepaws spread wide. Sniffing loudly, it tried to pinpoint where he was.

"I'm right here," Nate said, and bore in swinging. He sank the tomahawk into the monster's throat, the knife into its chest. A dark geyser spouted, splashing his face and throat, liquid warmer and stickier than the rain.

Abruptly, the grizzly's forelimbs closed around Nate. He was lifted into the air. He struggled mightily to break free but his sinews were puny compared to those of the grizzly.

Stories Nate had heard of trappers and mountain men crushed in bear hugs bore home the fact he was about to share their fate.

The grizzly opened its mouth to bite Nate's head. Jaws that could crush a human skull like an egg were poised to crush his, when shots rang out. Two, three, four blasts, one after the other.

Nate felt the bear stagger. He pushed against its chest but could not wrest loose. Someone shouted something he did not understand. He was conscious of falling, and after that, there was nothing, absolutely nothing at all.

Warmth revived him. Nate lay quietly, his eyes shut, remembering and sorting his thoughts.

"Will he die, Ma?" Evelyn asked, next to him.

"No, daughter. Your father is strong. He will mend. He will have many new scars but he will live." Winona's warm hand touched his.

"Just what he needs," Zach remarked. "More scars."

Nate opened his eyes. They were all there, ringing his bed. His wife and his daughter and his son and his son's wife and his best friend and his best friend's wife. Those he loved the most. Those he had fought to save. "Well," he said.

Squeals of delight and a chorus of whoops pealed. Evelyn threw her arms about him, tears streaming down her cheeks. "Oh, Pa! Pa!"

"Finally," Winona said huskily, and bending, she kissed him full on the mouth.

"How long?" Nate asked.

"You have been unconscious for more than two days," Winona informed him. "I have stitched all your wounds and applied salve and herbs."

"The grizzly?"

Zach grinned. "We ate some of it for supper. I wanted to make a rug but you cut the hide to ribbons."

Nate smiled at his wife. "How about something to eat? Bear stew sounds nice."

Shakespeare McNair came around the foot of the bed, sat on the edge, and placed a hand on Nate's shoulder. "So, Horatio," he said, the usual twinkle in his eyes, "what do you plan to train next? How about those wolverines? Or you could start with chipmunks and work your way up."

Nate King sighed.

#45
WILDERNESS
IN CRUEL CLUTCHES
David Thompson

Zach King, son of legendary mountain man Nate King, is at home in the harshest terrain of the Rockies. But nothing can prepare him for the perils of civilization. Locked in a deadly game of cat-and-mouse with his sister's kidnapper, Zach wends his way through the streets of New Orleans like the seasoned hunter he is. Yet this is not the wild, and the trappings of society offer his prey only more places to hide. Dodging fists, knives, bullets and even jail, Zach will have to adjust to his new territory quickly—his sister's life depends on it.

MAX BRAND®

FLAMING FORTUNE

The three novellas collected here showcase Max Brand's outstanding ability to create living, breathing characters whose unforgettable exploits linger long after the last page is turned. In "The Cañon Coward," you'll meet Harry Clonnell, a tracker who refuses to carry a gun and shuns violence yet has somehow earned the reputation of one of the most notorious bandits around. Outlaw Lefty Richards is put in quite a bind when his dying friend asks him to turn over his guns to the local sheriff in "A Wolf Among Dogs." And Speedy, one of Brand's most enduring characters, takes on the job of sheriff in "Seven-Day Lawman"—a job where no man has ever lasted longer than a week.

PARTNERS

PAUL BAGDON

His name is L. B. Taylor, but everyone in Burnt Rock, Texas, calls him Pound. They also call him the town drunk. Pound used to be a schoolteacher, but he traded in his job—and his self-respect—for a bottle a long time ago. All that's changing today. Today Pound made a new friend, a stranger in town named Zeb Stone, and Zeb is about to take Pound under his wing, pull him out of the gutter, and teach him a new career. Zeb is a shootist, a hired gun, who's looking for a partner. Pound is going to learn to live without booze, to ride, and to shoot. But he'll also learn the hard way that riding with a shootist is more dangerous than drowning in a bottle ever was!